A Runaway Train Novella

BY: KATIE ASHLEY

Music of the Soul

Copyright © 2013 by Katie Ashley

Smashwords Edition 2013

Edited by Marrion Archer | Making Manuscripts

Cover Designed by Letitia Hasser | RBA Designs

To **Cris Hadarly**—thanks for loving Jake and Abby as much as I do. You're the tiniest person yet greatest cheerleader I have! Thanks for supporting me and my books. Love you hard, girlie!!!

Acknowledgements

First and foremost thanks goes to **God** for all of his amazing blessing in my life the past year.

To my readers: I cannot thank you enough for your support and your love of my books. You are the most amazing blessing I have had in this business. Big, big hugs and love from me!

To Marion Archer—editor and plot magician extraordinaire—I couldn't make it without you. You bring so much to my books and make me a better writer and story-teller.

To Marilyn Medina: Your "eagle eyes" know no bounds, and I'm so thankful for getting to work with you, as well as your friendship. Golden Girls 4-Ever!

To Kim Bias: I can't thank you enough for talking me down from the ledge as well as making my books the best they can be. Thanks for the plot/blurb sessions. You do rock my socks!

To Shannon Furhman, Tammara Debbaut, Jen Gerchick, Jen Oreto, and Brandi Money: Thank you so much for being my "sluts" and working so hard to promote and support me. I can't tell you how much I appreciate it.

To my street team, **Ashley's Angels,** thank you so much for your support of me and my books.

To **Raine Miller and RK Lilley**: SCOLS 4-EVER! Thanks for your unfailing love and support in all areas personally and professionally. I couldn't ask for better friends and travel partners!

To the ladies of the Hot Ones: **Karen Lawson, Amy Lineaweaver, Marion Archer, and Merci Arellano,** thank you all for the laughter, the friendship, and the support. You're all amazing!!

Chapter One
"Jake"

I ducked my head under one of the low hanging oak trees as my feet crunched along the gravel pathway. The ache in my chest grew as I made the familiar pilgrimage through the garden of multicolored stones. Cool Springs Memorial Park was the last place on earth I wanted to be today, but my heart drove me there.

Close to the duck pond and beneath a massive oak tree was my mother's final resting place. "Hey Mama," I murmured, as I crouched down onto my knees on the grassy earth. The only reply I received was a few tweets from the birds nestled in the tree above me. "Brought you some flowers." Although the sun had yet to fade the bouquet of silk lilies on her headstone, I had still brought new ones. A smile crept on my lips as I went about replacing the flowers. I could almost hear her chiding me while a perfect picture of her with her hand on hip while wagging a finger at me formed in my mind. *"Jacob Ethan Slater, why on earth would you bring me new flowers when the ones I've got are perfectly good? Didn't I teach you a thing about managing finances?"*

"There. That looks better, doesn't it?" Cocking my head, I surmised the deep reds, oranges, and purples of the silk flower arrangement that I had just placed in the bronze vase on her marker. "Hope you like the fall flowers. Abby picked them out. Of course, if she was with me, she would know exactly how to reshape them and all, but I have no freakin' clue."

Although I felt like a tool doing it, I always spoke aloud to her when I came to visit her grave. It wasn't like I thought she could hear me—it was all part of my grief counseling. After her death when I had gone into a dark place, I had balked at seeing any professional therapists. I didn't feel right sharing my deepest, darkest thoughts and feelings with a stranger. So Abby had volunteered her mother's services. As the wife of a minister, Laura was used to consoling people. At times, I still felt guarded talking to her. She was the one who had given me the idea to talk to Mama to get my feelings out.

Rising to my feet, I wiped my dirty hands on my jeans. "I won't be back for a few weeks, but Papa is going to check in on you. You know, make sure your flowers are okay if it comes up a bad cloud, as he would say." Grinning at the thought of my grandfather and his Southern euphemisms, I brushed the back of my hand over my face. "Abby and I are leaving tomorrow for Mexico—we're getting married on some private beach there. I can't even begin to understand what she has planned. I'm just keeping my mouth shut and going along for the ride." Shaking my head, I smiled when I thought of how the office in my old house—now mine and Abby's— had been transformed into wedding planning central.

Gazing down at the marker, I sighed. "I know you'd be disappointed I wasn't getting married in a church, Mama. Trust me, Abby's parents totally flipped out that we weren't getting married at her dad's church. But this island is beautiful, and it gives us privacy from the paparazzi. We'll have the whole place to ourselves for a week—they only bring meals and do housekeeping when you call, and then they come by private boat. After the last few months of touring, I'm stoked as hell to have all that time alone with Abby."

I knew I was rattling on now to try and steady my out-of-control emotions, but somehow in some small way, it helped. A breeze rippled my clothing, and I shifted on my feet, fighting the tears that burned my eyes. "I'd give anything in the world if you could be there, Mama—for you to be sitting there in the first row wearing a beautiful dress." I shook my head and then wiped my eyes. I brought my fingers to my lips and kissed them. Then I reached down to touch her marker. "I love you as high as the sky," I murmured. With the familiar ache of grief burning in my chest, I turned and started making my way back to the truck.

It was hard to believe that almost two years had passed since my mother's death. Sometimes it seemed like forever since I had seen her smile, held her in my arms, and kissed her cheek. Then other times, her memory was so strong that it was like I expected to turn a corner in the house and see her there. Through the dark cloud of grief, I hadn't been the easiest person to be around or to love. Those first few months I drank too much, slept too much and generally acted like an asshole too much. But somehow Abby held on and wouldn't let go. Having proposed to her so many months ago, I couldn't wait to make her my wife.

But unfortunately, life had gotten in the way. Just as I was dealing with the implosion of my personal life, the band experienced an explosion of popularity. More was expected of us than ever before. Our crossover tour with Jacob's Ladder grew bigger and bigger, and we sold out more and more shows as we crisscrossed the country. Then came the Grammys eight months ago when we really found ourselves in the celebrity stratosphere.

Each and every time Abby and I tried to set a wedding date, another concert or appearance came up. I thought I was never going to get to make my angel Mrs. Jake Slater. But fortunately, we had finally found a one week window between the last leg of our tour and the holiday season, and in less than twenty-four hours, we would be exchanging vows on our own private beach in Mexico.

Just the thought sent a goofy grin curving on my lips. As I turned onto the road I'd called home for the last fifteen years, I threw up my hand to one of my older neighbors who sat on his front porch. While he waved back, I could only imagine he was grumbling about me and how I'd caused all the traffic on the one way, gravel road. Well, it wasn't entirely all me. Abby was to blame as well since it had been her idea to have a pre-wedding party at the farm.

When I pulled in the driveway, I found cars lining both sides of the road along with several catering trucks. I eased up beside the barn and hopped out. My dog, Angel, came yipping to my side. "Hey girl, you keepin' an eye on things for me?"

She barked and wagged her tail. I patted her head before I started back up the hillside. Down below the house where we usually held our bonfires, a huge, white tent had been erected. We were doing a sit-down dinner and dancing celebration for over two hundred people who would be unable to come to Mexico since it was a "destination wedding", as someone had called it. Tonight was mainly friends, extended family members, along with our road crew. Tomorrow was intended to be only our closest family and friends. Abby had wanted to keep the actual ceremony small with only fifty people in attendance. She claimed that she had to share me with so many people—the world when it came down to it—that on our special day, she wanted it to be as private as it could be.

As I started up the front walkway, the sweetest sound in the world floated back to me. Abby's singing. Although it was a part of my daily life when we were on tour, I never tired of hearing it. Without her voice, she would have never accidentally fallen into my bed for me to fall in love with. Craning my neck to find her, I jogged up the front steps.

Down at the far end of the porch, Abby sat cross-legged on the wicker couch with a guitar on her lap. Eli sat to her right in one of the rocking chairs. He strummed along with her, harmonizing on some of the lines. Gabe leaned back against the porch railing, tapping out the beat with his foot. Since we were coming right off our honeymoon to go back onto the road, I imagined they were trying to get in a little last minute rehearsal time.

Abby's eyes pinched shut in concentration, but as I made my way down the porch, they flew open as if she sensed my presence. Her gaze locked on mine as she sang the lyrics, "And I get lost in your eyes and thrilled at your touch. Nights like these were made for love."

With a smile, I winked at her. A pleased flush entered her cheeks as she continued singing. When she strummed the last chord, she glanced anxiously at me. It tugged at my heart that she always sought my approval when it came to her music. I nodded. "Very nice."

She gave me a beaming smile. "Thanks. It's a cover of an old song by The Lynns. We wanted to add a song or two to the set arrangement while we're writing the new stuff."

"Hmm, I knew it didn't sound too familiar."

Eli snorted. "The daughters of Loretta Lynn were the best compromise we could make with Abby that didn't involve busting out *Coal Miner's Daughter* or something hideous like that!"

I laughed as Abby scowled. "I can't help that I appreciate the greats of country music," she replied.

I grinned at her. "I'll agree with you on that one. I seem to remember some Dolly Parton karaoke in your past."

Abby grinned. "That's right." Glancing back at Eli, she said, "Be glad I'm not asking you to do a duet of *Islands in the Stream*."

"Over my dead body," he grumbled.

"You have nothing to worry about. I'm her only duet partner. Right, Angel?"

"No one but you—now and forever."

Gabe made a gagging noise behind us. "Why don't you guys get a room?" he suggested.

Eli shook his head. "Don't give them any ideas. That's all we need to send Mom completely over the edge—Abby late for the reception after a bang-fest."

When I opened my mouth to tell them to go fuck themselves, Abby distracted me by leaning in and peering at my watch. "Oh shit, it's after five? I've got to go get ready." She handed her guitar to Gabe before bridging the gap between us. Glancing back at her brothers, she then asked in a low voice, "Did you get your errand done?"

"Yes, I did."

She reached up on her tiptoes to plant a tender kiss on my lips. "I wish you would have let me go with you."

I shrugged. "Just something I needed to do. Besides, you had enough to do here."

Abby rolled her eyes. "Oh please. Between the wedding coordinator, the caterers and my mother, everything is taken care of. I seriously got shooed out of the kitchen when I tried to help. That's why I got the boys together to rehearse." A shudder rippled through her. "Too much nervous energy."

As she started into the house, I teasingly asked, "Having cold feet?"

She skidded to a stop before whirling back around to wrap her arms around my neck. "Never, ever, Mr. Slater. You're getting me as your lawfully wedded wife whether you like it or not."

I grinned. "Oh, I like it. In fact, I fucking love it."

"Good. I'm glad to hear that." She kissed me again before pushing out of my arms. "Okay, I gotta go get presentable for this pre-wedding shindig of ours." She eyed my ratty jeans and T-shirt. "I'd say the same for you, too."

"You're such a bossy thing."

With a wink, she replied, "Get used to it, babe."

A warm rush filled my chest as she started into the house. I didn't care if she bossed me around for the next fifty years, just as long as she was in my life. I'd never imagined loving anyone as much as I did Abby. Selflessly and unwaveringly, she had reached into the very darkest places of my soul to bring me back to the light. She'd shown me what the true, unfailing love of a good woman was. I would always owe her for loving me that much.

Close on her heels, the urge to show her just how much I loved and wanted her overcame me. My dick instantly swelled at the idea of being inside her. Just as she rounded the corner to go into the master bedroom, I grabbed her wrist, jerking her back to me. My other hand came around to press her body flush against mine. When

I ground myself into her core, her eyes bulged. "Jake, what are you—" she questioned breathlessly, before I crushed my lips to hers. My tongue danced along hers as I wrapped my arms tighter around her. Her little moan caused me to shiver.

When she felt my half-mast hard-on pressing into her stomach, she jerked away. "No, no, no!" she hissed. Her blonde ponytail flipped wildly back and forth as she shook her head at me. "We're abstaining until our wedding night, remember?"

I groaned. "You're the one who made that decision, not me."

"You agreed to it," she countered.

"Yeah, that was a week and a half ago when I was coming off of an all-day sexathon with you. I didn't realize what I was agreeing to."

Abby rolled her eyes. "It's only twenty-four more hours, Jake."

Reaching over, I nuzzled my lips against her neck. I wasn't playing fair since I knew it was one of her sensitive zones. A little sigh escaped her mouth when I ran my tongue across her jawline to suck on her earlobe. "I could explode by then."

"I just want our first time as man and wife to be special, that's all."

I pulled away to arch my brows at her. "Do you really think tomorrow night is going to be the most amazing sexual experience of your married life?"

She jerked her chin defiantly up at me. "Maybe," she countered.

My amused chuckle almost seemed to piss her off more. "Angel, we're going to be exhausted from tonight's party, jetlag, and the ceremony and reception. Bray and Lily didn't even have sex on their wedding night—they passed out into an exhausted coma." Taking her face in my hands, I grinned down at her. "By the flush on your cheeks and the way you just moaned into my mouth when I was kissing you, I can tell you *really* want to take me in that bedroom and have a quickie."

Abby chewed on her bottom lip, and I could tell her resolve was slowly fading. "It'll have to be fast. Everyone is supposed to be here at six."

"We can shower together—you know, multitask."

She grinned. "Oh, you say the most romantic things. Think you can whisper more sweet words in my ear?" she teased.

"Yeah, how about this? You're such a sweet looking smartass," I said before bringing my lips back to hers. Her eager tongue thrust into my mouth as she tightened her arms around my neck. Grabbing Abby by the ass, I hoisted her up and wrapped her legs around my waist. We both moaned at the closeness. With my lips locked on Abby's, I balanced her under the ass with one hand while my other groped blindly for the doorknob. When I finally found it, I flung it open and staggered into the room.

"Shit!" came a voice from the bed.

When my eyes flew open, I was a goner. One glance was all it took to kill my wood. On the bed, Mia scrambled to close the front of her shirt with one hand while she held Bella in her other arm. She pivoted on the bed, so her back was to us.

"Jesus," I groaned as I glanced down at my crotch. Just that one glimpse of AJ's breastfeeding fiancée was enough to completely obliterate my junk. My dick shriveled even further when Bella began shrieking and howling in protest that her meal had been interrupted.

Mia gave us an apologetic look over her shoulder. "I'm so sorry, guys. With all the catering staff and people buzzing around, I thought this would be the best place to feed her before we got dressed for the party. I should have gone in the bathroom."

"Oh, don't apologize, Mia," Abby said.

When I didn't respond, Abby elbowed me in the ribs. "Oomph," escaped my lips before I could stop myself. "Yeah, uh, it's fine," I replied. Gently, I set Abby down on her feet. I jerked my chin towards the bathroom. "You go on and get a shower. I'll use the one off the guest bedroom."

"You don't want me to come with you?" Abby asked coyly.

I scratched the back of my neck furiously. Part of me really wanted to shower with her, so we might finish what we started. But the other part was so traumatized that I knew there would be no way I'd be ready. "Um, no. I better take a rain check."

Abby's blue eyes widened in surprise. She stared at me for a moment before turning to Mia. "Excuse us," Abby said, as she grabbed my hand and led me into the bathroom. "What is wrong with you?"

With a shrug, I replied, "We were interrupted."

"It's never stopped you before." She cocked her head at me. "Did seeing Mia bother you that much?"

I couldn't help shuddering. "Yeah, it did."

"It's just a breast, Jake. I mean, you've seen your fair share of them."

"Not like that I haven't." At her amused expression, I threw up my hands. "That's my best friend's fiancée out there. I don't need a mental image of her boobs seared into my mind."

"You are too adorable," she said, before leaning up to kiss me.

"It's not funny," I argued feebly. When Abby's warm lips covered mine, I decided to shut the fuck up and not argue with her anymore. Knowing that she was trying to start something up again, I reluctantly pulled away. "You need to get ready."

"Are you sure?" When I nodded, she sighed. "Okay then. To be continued tomorrow night?"

I smiled. "Oh yes." I leaned over and pressed my lips to hers. "Love you."

"Love you, too," she murmured.

When I exited the bathroom, I kept my eyes glued to the hardwood floors. "Jake?"

Shit. It was AJ. "Yeah?" I questioned still not glancing up.

"What's this I hear about you ogling Mia's boobs?"

I jerked my head up to glare at him. "Excuse me?" I demanded.

Mia smacked AJ's arm. "You're such an ass!"

He grinned at her and then back at me. "I'm just screwing with you, man. Mia and I don't give two shits about what happened."

As I took a step toward him, he motioned down to where he balanced Bella on his hip. "Easy now."

"Using a baby as your shield? You're such a pussy." When I glanced at Bella, who was giving me a toothless smile, I grimaced. "Sorry for the p-word."

"It's okay. He deserved a lot worse," Mia replied with a grin.

"I gotta go get ready," I said, as I motioned to the door.

"I'll walk you out," AJ said. He glanced at Mia. "Do you need any help getting Bella ready?"

"We'll be fine. Of course, if you want to go get changed and come back to get her while I'm getting ready, that would be wonderful."

AJ smiled. "Anything for you, amorcito mio."

"Thanks, baby."

I snickered as I went out the door. "What?" AJ demanded behind me.

"I just never thought I would see the day that you were completely and totally whipped."

"Oh yeah, well, I could say the same damn thing about you," he countered.

I skidded to a stop in the hallway, causing AJ to bump into me. "Oh God, we've become the dudes we used to make fun of, haven't we?"

He winced. "Yeah, I think so."

With a sigh, I added, "We probably owe Brayden an apology for ragging his ass all these years."

AJ grinned. "Nah, no use in letting him know he was right. It'll just inflate his head even more."

Poking his head in the hallway, Brayden said, "I heard that, dickweeds."

"Dammit," I groaned, as we came into the living room.

Brayden rolled his eyes. "Whatever. Like I didn't already know I was right, and you two shitheads were wrong," he scoffed.

"Daddy, what's a shithead?" Melody asked.

As Brayden flushed, AJ and I busted out laughing. He glanced up to narrow his eyes at us. "Laugh now. Your time is coming." He pointed to AJ. "Especially you."

I laughed at AJ's grimace. I could only imagine he was thinking of how bad his potty-mouth was, along with Mia's. If Bella's first word was a cuss word, I wouldn't be surprised. "Well, on that note, I'm going to run upstairs and get ready. See you guys in a few?"

Brayden nodded while AJ replied, "Wouldn't miss it for the world."

After Jake left me partially sexed-up with no finish in the bathroom, I slipped into the cold shower that I knew was in order to get me through the night. As I lathered up my hair, I could barely contain the excitement that bubbled within me when I thought about my wedding day. I was probably most excited about the honeymoon, which for me wasn't just about the sex. It would be the first time that Jake and I were actually alone together. The last few months had been so hectic with our touring schedule. Since my brothers wanted to cut a new album, most of my free time was spent working on material with them. Even though I'd helped Jake write I'll Take You with Me, I still felt like a total and complete newbie when it came to songwriting. Luckily, Micah was willing to lend his skills to our cause.

While I was spending late nights at the studio, Jake and Runaway Train were also working on their next album. Considering the last one had been Grammy winning, the pressure was on to make the next album even bigger. So, between the touring and the albums, we rarely had time when it was just the two of us. And while we would only have a week alone together, I planned on making the most of every single second.

After I finished showering, I got out and toweled off. Grabbing my robe off the door, I slipped into the silky material. At the sound of a squeal in the bedroom, I grinned and padded over to the door. When I opened it, I saw Bella on the bed with Mia bent over her. As Mia blew raspberries on Bella's naked belly, Bella giggled and kicked her feet. Mia pulled away to cock her head. "Now can we put on your pretty dress without you pitching a hissy fit?"

Bella replied with a coo and a wave of her arms. Mia glanced over her shoulder at me. "I'm putting her in the one you gave her at her baptism."

I smiled. "She'll look beautiful in it, I'm sure." I had been both surprised and honored when Mia and AJ had asked me to be Bella's godmother. I felt there were other more deserving family members, especially AJ's sister. But Mia had insisted. So four months ago, I'd stood with AJ's brother, Antonio, at the altar of Christ the King as Bella was baptized. Among several gifts I'd gotten her was a dress I'd hoped she'd be wearing to her parent's rehearsal dinner since it was lacy and frilly. But it looked like she was going to be debuting it at mine since Mia and AJ weren't getting married for another four months.

"Sorry about Jake freaking out like that on you," I said, as I toweled my hair.

Mia adjusted the enormous lavender bow on Bella's head. "It's okay. I'm surprised it didn't happen to him sooner like it did to Rhys when we were out on tour."

"Oh no. Did he have a similar reaction?"

Mia laughed. "Worse. He ran into the wall trying to get away from me."

"Seriously?" I asked.

"Sadly, yes." With a smile, she shook her head. "Men spend their lives being obsessed with boobs, and then the moment a baby is attached to it, they lose their minds."

I grinned. "I know, right?"

"Well, when it's all said and done, I'm really, really sorry that I interrupted you two." She winked at me. "You guys looked pretty hot and heavy there."

"It's okay." When Mia gave me a "yeah right" look, I shook my head. "Trust me, it was fine. Besides, Jake was trying to break my resolve on abstaining until our wedding night."

Mia's dark brows furrowed in confusion. "Excuse me?"

"Oh, I decided to make our wedding night special, we wouldn't have sex for a week before the wedding."

"Hmm, maybe I should torture AJ with that in a few months."

I laughed. "Why not?"

She grinned. "Considering we've already done everything backwards, I don't think we need to worry about our wedding night being very special. In the end, you make your special moments, and they usually happen when you go off the script."

"The script?"

"Oh, you know. The life script—the way you've meticulously planned out how everything is going to happen in your life." Mia picked up Bella. As she stared into her daughter's face, pure love emanated in her eyes. "My life script never would have ever included AJ. I mean, a rock star? Who in their right mind would want to marry someone who lives a rootless existence on the road with beautiful women constantly throwing themselves at their feet?"

She snorted. "Not me, that's for damn sure. But that's where I was wrong. And when I decided to just screw the script, that's when I found the truest of loves and the greatest of happiness."

"I see what you mean." I'd been pretty rigid with my life script lately, and I couldn't help wondering if it was for the best. "Maybe I should go to Jake tonight after the party," I murmured.

Mia adjusted Bella on her hip. "And finish what you started?" she asked with a sly smile.

"Oh yes."

She grinned. "I think that sounds like a wonderful idea." She then motioned to the bathroom. "Now go finish getting ready so you can put this plan in motion."

I laughed. "Yes, ma'am," I replied, before hurrying to the closet for my dress.

At a few minutes past six, Jake and I made our way down the hillside to the tent. It was already teeming with people as waiters in white jackets hurried about serving hors d'oeuvres. With a champagne flute in my hand, I weaved in and out of the tables as I tried to greet each and every one of our guests. "Don't you look like a living dream?" Frank complimented when I came to the table full of Runaway Train roadies and their families.

I glanced down at my dress. I had picked a white, strapless, Grecian-styled dress with a glittering bodice for tonight's party. Around my throat were Susan's pearls. As I turned to the side, I asked, "You like it?"

"It's beautiful, but you're even more beautiful in it."

"Aw, you're too sweet." I leaned over and kissed his cheek, which earned hoots and hollers from the men.

"Hey, now, save some loving for me," Jake teased from behind us.

"Fine, fine, you can have some too," I replied, before kissing his cheek.

"Thanks, Angel," Jake murmured with a wink. As he stayed joking with the guys, I moved on since dinner would be served promptly at seven. While I chatted and laughed with friends and family, there was one table that I kept putting off going to, and that was the one where Jake's father and stepmother were seated. Taking a long gulp of my champagne, I bit the bullet by plastering on my best smile.

"Hey, how are you guys?"

Jake's stepmother, Nancy, returned my smile. "Great, thank you. Don't you look exquisite?"

"Thank you."

"I can't wait to see what your dress looks like tomorrow," Nancy said.

"It's a little more poofy than this one," I replied with a smile. When I turned to address Jake's dad, Mark, he stared expectantly at me.

"Can I talk to you for a moment?" Mark asked.

I couldn't help nibbling on my bottom lip before I responded. "Um, sure."

When he rose out of his chair, I couldn't hide my surprise. "I thought it would be better to discuss this alone," he said in a low voice.

"Okay," I replied. With his hand at the small of my back, Mark eased me away from the crowded tables to the outside of the tent. He made sure we were out of earshot from the others before he spoke. "Abby, I just want you to know that I couldn't be more pleased that Jake has found a girl like you to settle down with."

"Thank you," I said, hesitantly. I knew from his tone and expression, there was a lot more Mark wanted to say.

With a ragged sigh, he gave me a tight smile. "Because of the woman you are, I know if there's anyone who can mend the relationship between myself and Jake, it's you."

My eyes widened. "I think you flatter me a little too much."

"Jake values your opinion more than anyone else's. Ever since Susan died, he's cut himself off even further from me." He shook his head sadly. "I'll be the first to admit that I've made mistakes in my life. But I love my son, and I want to be a part of his life. Please, Abby, please try and talk to Jake."

My heart ached for Mark as he stood pleading in front of me. "I don't know what I can do—" When Mark opened his mouth to protest, I held up my hand. "But I will try. I promise you that."

"You will?"

"Yes. I want peace and happiness for Jake in all areas of his life, including you. Someday when we have children, I want you to have a part in their lives."

Tears shimmered in Mark's eyes. "Thank you. That means so much to me."

He reached over and gave me a quick hug. When he pulled away, he glanced over my shoulder with a smile. "Evening, son."

"Evening," Jake replied.

"I apologize for stealing your beautiful bride-to-be for a few minutes."

"It's fine." I inwardly cringed at the coolness of Jake's tone.

"I'm looking forward to the wedding tomorrow. Allison is really excited to be a bridesmaid."

"We're happy to have her. She's such a sweetheart," I said.

Mark swayed on his feet, and I could tell there was more he wanted to say. "Well, I'll leave you two lovebirds."

"Goodnight," I said.

He turned to go but waited until Jake finally replied, "See ya."

As Mark walked away, Jake wrapped his arms around my waist. He nuzzled my neck with his warm lips before asking, "What did he want?"

"Just to talk."

"Mmm, hmm."

"He loves you, Jake." When I felt him tense behind me, I quickly added, "He wants nothing more than to mend the broken fences, so that you two can have a real relationship."

Jake snorted. "Too many years and too much shit have passed between us."

Turning in his arms, I brought my hand to his cheek. "It's never too late for forgiveness."

His brows shot up at my words. "And just whose side are you on?"

"Yours." I emphasized my words by drawing myself close to his chest. "I'm always on your side, and you know that."

He kissed the top of my head. "I don't know, Abby. Some things are better left the way they are."

Pulling away, I stared into his face. "Just promise me that you'll try a little harder where your dad is concerned."

A defeated growl came from his chest. "Fine. I'll try."

"Thank you," I said, before bestowing a kiss on his lips.

"Come on. Let's go eat."

"Sounds good to me." I let Jake take my hand and lead me through the crowd to the table at the head of the tent. It was for us and our wedding party. As the catering staff bustled around serving the first course, Jake picked up the microphone off the table.

"Everyone," he began. When people kept talking, he tapped the top of the microphone. "Helloooo? Can you guys hear me out there?"

At the top of his lungs, AJ shouted, "Hey everybody, shut the fuck up!"

When there was only dead silence, Jake shook his head and grinned. "Thanks, buddy."

"Anytime," AJ replied with a wink.

"Yeah, so, I'm not one for speeches and shit like that, but I did want to take a second before everyone started stuffing their faces to say thank you from both myself and Abby for being with us on the eve before the big day. Everyone in this room is family, whether we're related by blood or by a business or personal relationship. You've seen us through some tough times over the last few years, and we can never forget how your love and support stayed consistent through the bad times, as well as the good." He turned to me and smiled. "Most of all, I hope you're with us for many more to come. So thank you very, very much."

"Now let's eat!" AJ exclaimed banging his fist on the table.

Jake rolled his eyes. "As the caveman said, let's eat." As applause rang out around us, Jake eased down into the chair beside me. Although my nerves were working in overdrive, my stomach was not affected. I couldn't wait to finally eat what I had picked out so many months ago. Plus, I had been eating as little as possible in that week or so to get into my dress. All my willpower seemed to go out the window when the Caesar salad came. I dug in like a woman who hadn't eaten in weeks. "Pace yourself, Angel," Jake joked.

"I can't help it, I'm starving," I mumbled through the mouthful of bread I had just stuffed in.

Jake grinned. "I'm so glad I'm marrying a woman with an appetite."

"You might not be saying that for long, especially if I can't get into my dress tomorrow afternoon."

He snorted. "I highly doubt that." He leaned over to where his warm lips brushed against my earlobe. "Besides, more of you is just more to love, especially loving your delicious curves in the bedroom."

"Hmm, we'll see if you keep that attitude when I get pregnant and put on fifty pounds."

Jake stiffened beside me. I had found the right words to cool his advances. Although he loved cuddling with Bella or playing with Jude and Melody, Jake was still gun-shy about the idea of us having children. When anyone mentioned us having kids, he would scoff at the idea. He claimed we had at least two more American tours and a world tour to get through before he even thought of knocking me up. With the world tour scheduled to take off in a year, I had a feeling even after that, he still wouldn't be ready. There was something deep inside him that didn't feel like he was capable of being a father. Thinking that was how he felt broke my heart. He had so much love to give a child. I wanted more than anything for him to be able to see that, but I didn't want to press the issue now. We had time to work on it.

I guess he sensed my sadness at his reaction because he kissed my cheek tenderly. "We'll have to wait and see, Angel."

Satisfied with his answer, I smiled at him. "I'll hold you to it."

With a wink, he said, "Sounds like a plan."

Two courses of mouthwatering food later, AJ stood up and took the microphone. "Oh Jesus," Jake muttered.

"As you know, it's customary for the best man to make a speech at the wedding reception. Since some of you won't be with us tomorrow, I felt it was best to give my speech now, so no one missed out." AJ flashed a wide grin. "When I was twelve years old, a family moved next door to us. While I went over to be friendly and introduce myself, I really just wanted to get a better view of the hot chick." He glanced out into the audience. "Sorry, Andrea, but it's the truth."

"Oh please," she muttered, while burying her head in her hands.

"Anyway, while on my chick-seeking mission, I found out that there was a kid my age who would be visiting every other weekend. I was pretty stoked at that news 'cause at the time, I thought if I made nice with the dude, then I would be around more to see his step-sister."

"You're such an ass," Jake muttered with a grin.

"So, the first weekend Jake came out of the boonies to visit his dad, I went over to meet him. I had no idea that day I was meeting my new best friend. I mean, it certainly wasn't too memorable. We sat around eating junk food and playing video games. No, it was the next day that our fates were sealed when Jake brought out his guitar. While he wanted to sing and play some hokey Johnny Cash shit his grandfather had taught him, I quickly took him downstairs to the basement where my drums were. I guess you could say it was then and there our true and unfailing bromance began."

As everyone laughed, AJ turned to me and winked. "Over the years of watching Jake the Lady Killer in action, I knew it was going to take a special girl to snag his heart and make him toe the line. One who was feisty and sassy, sweet and kind, beautiful and sexy, and his creative and musical equal. And then one day, this woman..." he pointed at me. "This gorgeous woman right here literally fell into his bed and didn't take his bullshit. Ever."

I groaned but smiled in spite of myself. "Thanks for bringing that up in front of everybody."

"You're welcome," he replied. As he cocked his head at me, a mischievous twinkle entered his dark eyes. "You know at first, I kinda hoped that maybe this beautiful little firecracker and myself might be meant to Tango into the sunset together. But no, it was clear almost from the very beginning that she was meant for only Jake. I'm just honored to call her a friend and musical collaborator. But best of all, tomorrow I will get to call her my best friend's wife."

"Oh, AJ," I murmured, as my hand came to my throat.

"His ball and chain for now until the day he dies," he added with a grin.

I laughed and shook my head at him as he picked up his champagne flute. "So, I ask you to raise a glass to the couple of the evening, the man and woman of the hour, and along with me, wish them all the blessings, joy, and happiness that life can bring." He thrust his drink into the air. "To Jake and Abby."

"To Jake and Abby," the crowd recited, as they lifted their glasses.

Jake clinked my glass with his before dipping his head to kiss me. "Here's to us, Angel," he murmured, against my lips.

"To us," I replied breathlessly. I brought the crystal flute to my lips and took a sip while Jake downed his in one gulp. "Now who needs to pace himself?" I teasingly asked.

"What do you say we dance?"

I couldn't help laughing. "Seriously? You hate to dance."

"With anyone else, yes. But with you, I'd love to."

"If you're sure…"

"I'm positive."

"Okay, then." I slipped my hand into his and let him pull me out of my chair. We made our way in front of the main table where a wooden floor had been erected for dancing. Across from us, a band had been tuning up. Jake gave a nod to the lead singer—a tall, lanky guy with shaggy dark hair.

"Okay, everyone, I have a special request from the groom-to-be. It's an oldie…actually one we weren't even familiar with, but since Jake wants us to play it, then by God we're doing it." Glancing over his shoulder, he then counted off.

Instantly, I recognized the song. It was one Jake had on his iPod under a playlist called My Angel. It was from the 90s, if you considered that an oldie, and it was called *How Do You Talk to an Angel?*

Jake smiled down at me. "Good choice?"

"Oh, yes."

"I thought you'd like it."

Tomorrow my brothers would be reuniting with Micah to do the singing at the ceremony and the reception. Tonight had been up to Jake. "So, I don't think I ever asked who the band is?"

"It's Brayden's cousin, Cade's." A sheepish look entered Jake's face. "Remember the second night you were on the bus with us when the guys and I were supposed to go hear a band play, but I got wasted, puked on you, and passed out?"

I quirked my brows at him. "How could I ever forget?"

Jake laughed. "Yeah, thought you would. Of course, I kinda hoped you would also remember that was the night I truly came clean with you, and that I wanted a chance to win you over."

"I remember that, too."

"Good," he murmured, before kissing me.

As the song faded to an end, Jake and I remained lip-locked under the twinkling lights of the tent. I could have stayed in that moment forever—wrapped in his arms, feeling the intensity of his love with each and every kiss. In the end, I just hoped to be able to bottle up a little of the feeling, so that when there were hard times or fights or when I felt like his love had waned, I could look back on this moment in time and know how truly and deeply we loved each other. It was true bliss and heaven on earth.

Only the sound of a rumbling explosion caused me to pull away. Over Jake's shoulder, the night sky lit up in a multi-colored array. I gasped. "Fireworks?"

Jake grinned. "A little surprise."

People abandoned their chairs and walked outside of the tent. "Too redneck?" Jake asked, as he slid his arm around my waist.

I laughed. "No, I love it."

"I figured you were used to big finales during our shows, so I thought our party needed a big moment."

"They're amazing. I mean, they're as good as the ones at Stone Mountain on the Fourth of July!"

"I'm glad you think so," Jake mused as we tilted our heads to take in the display.

When the last streaks of color followed a sonic boom, Jake took my hand and brought it to his lips. "How about we cut that cake now?"

"That sounds good to me."

As we waved goodbye to the last guest, Jake peeked at his watch. "Wow, I'm impressed. Everyone ate, danced, and drank and were outta here by eleven thirty."

"That's because there weren't many Italians or Mexicans here," AJ commented with a grin. "We party until the sun comes up. Don't we, Mia?"

Mia nodded. "Yep, it's true."

I laughed. "Then I better start training for your wedding."

"Oh, it's going to be epic for sure," AJ remarked.

"Well, considering we have a slammed day tomorrow, I'm kinda glad that everyone decided to go home a little early," I said.

"It was a nice party though, wasn't it?" Jake remarked, as we started up the porch steps.

"It was beautiful—everything I hoped it would be," I said.

With a smile, Jake said, "Best of all, we get to party more tomorrow."

Mia glanced down at Bella, who was sound asleep in her arms. "I better get this pumpkin to bed." When AJ started to ease down on the sofa, Mia grabbed his shirt sleeve. "I could use a little help."

AJ grinned. "Is that code for you want me to come downstairs so you can have your way with me?"

At Mia's laugh, Bella stirred, so Mia quickly covered her mouth with her free hand. "Yeah, Mr. Latin Lover, that's exactly what I was thinking," she replied softly.

"Mmm, good deal." With a wave of his hand to us, he added, "Night bitches," before following Mia to the basement stairs. Glancing over her shoulder at me, Mia winked, causing a flush to enter my cheeks.

Trying to recover before Jake got suspicious, I asked, "Think our house guests will think we're poor hosts if we go on to bed?"

Jake shook his head. "I think your parents and brothers understand. And from the sound of it, AJ and Mia are covered."

"I think so," I replied with a smile.

"So I guess this is goodnight, huh?"

I nodded. "Yep, the last night we'll ever spend as single people."

Cocking his head, Jake asked, "Remind me again why I didn't have a swinging bachelor party?"

I smacked his arm playfully. "Because you're marrying an insecure, overbearing shrew who couldn't stand the thought of some fake-breasted, plastic Barbie giving you a lap dance?"

A wicked gleam burned in Jake's blue eyes. "Actually, I think it was more that I was a caveman who didn't want some oiled dude in a banana hammock dry humping you."

"Ew!" I cried while wrinkling my nose.

"I'm sure that with some hot, cute little number like yourself, all the Magic Mike douchebags would have wanted to rub up on you."

"I would have totally declined since I'm very happy having you, and only you, rub up on me."

Jake's amused expression grew serious as he traced my cheekbone with his thumb. "Are you sure?"

My eyes widened. "Excuse me? Am I sure about gross, oily male strippers?"

He laughed. "No, I meant about me and only me."

"Considering we're getting married tomorrow, I think that shows I'm pretty damn sure."

"But are you sure you're okay with me being the only man you've ever slept with." His brows furrowed in thought. "I mean, do you think you'll look back one day and wish you'd had more experience?"

I shook my head furiously from side to side. "Never, ever." Sliding my arms around his neck, I smiled. "I can't ever imagine anyone being a better lover than you."

"And since you have no one else to judge that by, I don't—"

Bringing my hand to his chest, I silenced him. "Don't go there, Jake. I know what I've felt with you, and I don't want anyone else. I'm fully satisfied that you will be the only man I sleep with for the rest of my life."

Although I wasn't entirely sure he believed me, a pleased smile curved on his lips. "I'm satisfied that you're the last woman I'll ever sleep with for the rest of my life."

"I sure hope so."

"Give me a goodnight kiss, future ball and chain," he teased.

I leaned up on my tiptoes to bring my mouth to his. He snaked his arms around my waist, drawing me flush against him. As I deepened the kiss by thrusting my tongue against his, Jake's fingers came to tangle in the bottom strands of my hair. He tasted sweet like the chocolate cake we had fed each other for dessert.

When I pulled away, Jake groaned. "Yeah, guess we better cut that out for tonight."

I bit my lip to keep from smiling since I knew what I was going to do as soon as the house was quiet, and I was sure everyone was asleep. "See you tomorrow then," I said.

"Night, Angel. I love you."

"I love you, too."

Jake gave me a chaste kiss on the lips before heading out the front door. Fighting the butterflies in my stomach, I made my way down the hall to the bedroom. Although I slipped out of my dress and into my pajamas, I had no intention of going to sleep. Instead, I lay in bed, listening to the sounds around me.   Long after the last footsteps could be heard pattering down the hall or the sound of water in the pipes, I finally threw back the covers and hopped out of bed.

I knew exactly what I wanted to wear, and it only took two seconds to pull it out of my suitcase. I then slipped into the bathroom and got dressed. As soon as I was done, I crept out of the bedroom and down the hall. I could hear my dad snoring in the guest bedroom, while the sound of muted TV came from the office where Eli and Gabe were sleeping on an air mattress and the pullout couch. Grabbing a flashlight out of the hall closet, I then snuck out the front door. I jogged as fast as I could in my robe and slippers across the front lawn and down the hill. Thankfully, Angel had actually listened to me when I told her to stay on the porch. The last thing I needed was for her to start a barking marathon and alert everyone that I was running around half-naked outside.

When I got to the barn, I reached under one of the potted plants to get out the hide-a-key. Gently, I unlocked the door and stepped inside. When I closed the door behind me, I heard rustling in the bed upstairs. Without hesitation, I made my way across the living room toward the stairs. Of course, I didn't expect Jake to have left his shoes in the middle of the floor, causing me to trip and bang into the ladder.

"Ow!" I cried before I could bite down on my lip.

"Abby?" Jake questioned. Within a few seconds, he was peering over the railing of the loft.

Gazing up at him, I teased, "Yes, it's me. Were you expecting someone else?"

His brows furrowed. "I wasn't expecting anyone, especially you."

"Well…surprise!"

Jake gave me a funny look as I started climbing the stairs. When I got to the top rung of the ladder, he helped me off. "What are you doing here?"

To answer his question, I undid the tie on my robe. I then shimmied it off my shoulders and let it fall to the floor. Jake's eyes widened while his mouth gaped open at my skimpy lingerie. "Abby..."

"Do you remember this?" I asked, running my hand over the silky material.

As the revelation washed over him, desire burned in his eyes. "You were wearing that the night we made love for the first time."

"Yes, I was." Stepping forward, I wrapped my arms around his neck. "I want you to finish what you started earlier this afternoon. But most of all, I want you to make love to me again on our wedding eve in the same place we first came together."

Jake's gaze left mine to momentarily flicker over to the clock on the nightstand. "But it's after midnight. That means it's our wedding day. What about the bad luck?"

"We make our own luck. But more than anything, we make our own memories, and I want to make one with you tonight."

As his arms wrapped tighter around me, he cocked his head at me. "Trust me, Angel, I certainly don't want to argue with you. I just don't want you to regret it later."

"There hasn't been a single moment I've regretted with you."

Jake's brows rose in surprise. "Really?"

"I promise."

He smiled. "I'm really glad to hear that."

"So are you down with my plan?"

"Oh, hell yeah," he said, as he backed us over to the bed.

"Since when do you wear T-shirts to sleep in?" I asked.

He grinned. "I found the more clothes I had on, the better I reigned myself in."

"Oh no, has our abstaining caused you to spend a little extra time with your hand?" I teased.

"I refused to rub one out, which is why I'm wearing the clothes, instead of sleeping naked."

"Poor baby," I murmured. Taking the hem of his T-shirt, I had to stand on tiptoes to whisk it over his head. Once I tossed it onto the floor, I went for the waistband of his boxers. As my fingers skimmed along his abdomen, I glanced up. His hands remained at his sides, rather than ripping off my clothes like he usually did. "Is this how we're playing it? You naked and me in my lingerie?"

He grinned. "Maybe." His hand came to cup my breasts through the lacy fabric. "Maybe seeing you in this number gets me so hot that I want to enjoy it as long as possible."

"Hmm, that's nice." After I shoved the fabric over his hips, I was rewarded with a sight of how ready he was for me. Dropping to my knees, I leaned forward to bestow a kiss on the crown of his head. His abdominal muscles clenched. As I pushed his boxers down to the floor, I kissed a slow, tedious trail over his calves and thighs. "Angel," Jake pleaded.

Deciding to put him out of his misery, I took his length in my hand. At his sharp intake of breath, I slid my fingers up and down his erection. Jake eyes burned with lust as he stared down at me with hooded eyes. Licking my lips, I brought my mouth to him and sucked his length inside. Jake's deep groan reverberated around the bedroom. He swept my hair aside to watch what I was doing to him. "Fuck, you drive me wild," he murmured. I kept sucking him harder and deeper while pumping my hand up and down.

Just as I felt him begin tensing up, he jerked away from me, and his erection fell free of my mouth. With gentle hands, he lifted me off my knees. His hands went to the hem of my nightie, and he lifted it over my head. As one hand came to cup my breast, the other went to jerk down my thong. "Easy now. Don't rip it, caveman," I admonished him with a smile.

"You'd like it if I did."

"Oh I would?"

His head bobbed up and down. "You like it when I take control." His thumb flicked over my nipple, causing me to gasp.

"Not bad," I murmured.

When both of his hands came to pinch my nipples, moisture flooded my core, and I couldn't help moaning. He then eased onto his back on the bed. Taking my hand, he jerked me over to where I was straddling him. He then pulled me further up his body until his mouth connected with my core. "Oh God," I moaned, as Jake's tongue dipped inside me. With his hands clamped tight to my thighs, his mouth continued a steady assault. My breathing became erratic, and I pitched forward to grab hold of the headboard. My hips moved in time with the thrusting of his tongue inside me. Unable to grip the headboard for long, my hands felt blindly along the side of the bed. Jake's grip on my thighs released, and his hands clasped with mine. As I squeezed his fingers with my own, I continued riding his face and tongue. A powerful orgasm rippled through me, causing me to throw my head back and scream his name.

I was still riding the pulsing waves of my orgasm when Jake slid me down the length of his body and then impaled me on his erection. With his hands gripping my hips, he began working me on and off of him. Each time I came back down, he thrust his hips up to meet me. I splayed my palms flat across his pecs, but his hands seemed to be everywhere. Tangling through the strands of my hair, cupping my breasts, sliding up and down my back—his touch was all over me, and it drove me deliciously wild into sensory overload.

He pushed himself into a sitting position and wrapped his arms around me. We were now chest to chest, face to face and eye to eye. I shivered with pleasure at the feel of more of his skin brushing against mine. The fine, dark hairs on his chest tweaked and teased my nipples as we rubbed against each other. As he brought his mouth to mine, his tongue plunged in and out in the same rhythm. After sliding a hand between us, his fingers stroked my swollen clit, and I came again, shouting his name and clinging desperately to his broad shoulders. As I started coming down, Jake continued pumping in and out of me. When I sensed he was getting close, I pulled back. I wanted to be looking into his eyes when he went over the edge.

"Abby," he moaned, as his hips jerked, and his body shuddered in release. When he was finished, he remained buried inside me. He lay back on the bed, taking me with him.

As I snuggled into his side, I sighed with contentment. "That was…"

"Amazing. As always."

I grinned as I propped my head up on my elbow. "Do you think it'll always be like this?"

"You mean, after we've been married for twenty years and you've popped out a kid or two, will we still be having sex as hot as this?"

"Yeah."

"I sure as hell hope so," he replied, with a grin.

"Me too."

"Sweet dreams, Angel."

"Only of you," I murmured, before I closed my eyes and fell into a contented sleep.

Chapter Three
"Jake"

As the sun streamed in through the wide window panes, it warmed my body under the sheets. I'd been awake long before dawn. I'd savored the feel of Abby wrapped in my arms. In the quiet, I listened to her sleeping, the sweet little snores she emitted. There was nothing quite like holding my girl as she slept—the feel of her soft curves pressing into my body. I don't think I ever felt safer and more secure than I have with her by my side.

At the same time, my mind had also been preoccupied. The telltale signs of a new song waiting to be written flickered through my subconscious. It had started out small—a few jumbled words, a few chords. And then as I came awake, it built and built. In a low voice, I hummed a melody—one that was now playing on loop through my mind. Beneath the sheet, my foot began tapping out the rhythm. My eyes snapped open. Now that I truly had it, I didn't want to lose it. Fumbling with the sheets and comforter, I threw them off and bolted from the bed.

Abby raised her head and gazed at me with drowsy eyes. "Jake, where are you going?"

"I have to get my guitar."

"Seriously, I don't need a wedding day serenade," came her muffled reply, as she burrowed deeper under the covers.

I snorted. "Sorry to burst your bubble, but that's not it, Angel." I threw open the closet door and turned on the light. Most of my good guitars, or the ones I preferred, were up at the main house. I would have to make do with my Papa's old Gibson.

When I returned to the bed, Abby sat cross-legged with the sheet clutched around her breasts. The sunshine streaked across her body, making her skin glow. "Damn, you're so beautiful."

A flush entered her cheeks. "Thank you," she murmured.

As I eased closer to her, I said, "I woke up to a melody in my head."

"Really?"

"Mmm, hmm." I leaned over to open the nightstand for a pen and pad. Then I started scribbling down some of the chords that had been floating through my mind. Once I had those down, I propped my guitar on my legs. As I began strumming the melody I'd heard so clearly in my head, I closed my eyes to let the lyrics that were jumbled in my mind unfurl. I cleared my throat *and began to sing.*

"When you fell into my life, I was shattered beyond repair.

But as the shining angel of redemption, you didn't seem to care.

While the tempest swirled around me, you led me to solid ground.

You're the purest, deepest love a man like me has ever found.

There is a fire that burns within me that only you can ignite.

You're the light that fills my soul in the darkest, bleakest night.

You're the balm that cures the wound; the lifeline in the storm.

You are the song of my heart, the music of my soul."

Abby blinked a few times. "It's...amazing."

"You think?"

"No, I *know* it is. I can't believe you woke up with that in your head."

"Let's just say I had an inspiring night," I commented, before winking at her.

A flush filled her cheeks as she ducked her head. Even with Abby's vote of confidence, I felt there was still something missing in the song. It needed a deeper layer to make it have even more feeling. And I was looking right at that beautifully naked and disheveled layer.

When she glanced up again, Abby's eyes widened. "Why are you staring at me?" she questioned softly.

"I'm trying to decide what your part is."

Her brows rose in surprise. "I have a part?"

I smiled. "You shouldn't even have to ask. You have a part in every single thing in my life, Angel. You're every word in this song—every note. Only the purest and sweetest melody could be inspired by you."

"Oh Jake," she murmured, as tears welled in her deep blue eyes. Before I knew it, she had closed the gap between us and thrown herself into my arms. My guitar made a screeching noise as her warm lips met mine in a frenzied kiss. "I love you so much it hurts."

"I know. I feel the same way."

Pushing her hair away from her face, I then brought my lips back to hers. I wanted nothing more than to stay in that moment forever with the most important things in my life—my love, my guitar, and my music. But the sound of the front door bursting open caused me to pull away. It took only seconds for AJ's booming voice to echo throughout the loft. "Yo, twatcake, are you up and at em? We leave for the airport in half an hour."

I groaned. "It's always an interruption, isn't it?"

Abby giggled. "Sometimes I think I'm not just marrying you, but the boys, too. I mean, they're so much a part of our lives."

"Yeah, well, just remember you're mine and only mine, got it?"

She kissed my cheek. "Yes, Mr. Possessive."

With a wink, I said, "And don't you forget it."

AJ bounded over the side of the ladder, causing Abby to squeal and grab for the sheet. "Oh shit, I'm sorry," he said, before whirling around.

"It's okay." Once she was wrapped as tight as a mummy in the sheet, she hopped off the bed and ran into the bathroom.

When the door closed, AJ turned around. He held up his hands. "I swear I didn't know she was here."

"It's okay, man."

"By the way, her mom is looking for her."

"Oh shit," Abby moaned from the bathroom.

I laughed. "You're about to be a married woman, and you're still worried about your mother?"

She poked her head out the door. "I'll never be too old or too married not to worry about my mother." She glanced at AJ. "Quick, get me a pair of Jake's sweats and a T-shirt."

"Why?"

Abby rolled her blue eyes. "Because I'm going to pretend I went out for a walk this morning to clear my head. The last thing my mother, least of all my father, needs to know is that I just spent the night with Jake."

"Got it," AJ replied, before heading to the closet. When he returned, he thrust some clothes at Abby.

"Thank you," she replied, as she slammed the door.

"You don't think they're going to wonder why you're wearing my clothes that are about two sizes too big for you?" I asked.

"I'll say it's because I missed you and wanted to be close to you. That also covers us if they smell you on me," came her muffled reply behind the door.

AJ grinned. "She's good. If we ever need an alibi, she's our girl."

Then Abby appeared from out of the bathroom. Her former bed hair had been tamed into a ponytail. She leaned over the bed to kiss me. "I love you, and I'll see you this afternoon."

"Yep, sunset on the beach. You'll be the one in the veil, and I'll be the one forced to wear a pink vest."

"Hey, at least you don't have to wear a full tux or suit," she argued.

"Guess you're right. But damn, Angel. Did you really have to choose pink?"

She gave me a teasing wink. "I'm a true steel magnolia, so of course, I wanted some blush and bashful in my wedding."

My brows furrowed. "What the hell are you talking about?"

"Don't worry about it. See you later." She grinned and blew me a kiss before hightailing it down the ladder.

When the door slammed behind her, I tossed the notebook at AJ. "Got us a new hit."

As he glanced over the lyrics, he bobbed his head. "Abby inspired, I presume."

"Oh, yeah."

"Brayden will be glad to hear it. He's feeling the pressure of the new album."

"I have a feeling I might get even more inspired on my honeymoon."

AJ grinned. "I say go for it. Just make sure you take the time to enjoy yourself."

Throwing back the covers, I started for the bathroom. "Oh, I plan on enjoying myself several times a day," I replied with a wink.

Chapter Four
"Abby"

The main suite of the island's house teemed with people. As nervous energy hummed through every fiber of my being, it took everything I had to sit still in the chair in front of the mirror. It still felt surreal that I was even here—that after hopping a plane and then taking a boat, I was in my own island paradise. I'd been dreaming of this day my entire life, and now it was finally here.

To combat my nervousness, I'd been tapping my foot restlessly while Marion, the band's makeup and hair stylist, went about transforming me. When she started in with the eyeliner, she gave me an exasperated look. "Would you stop with the tapping, or you're going to look like some Goth chick."

"Sorry."

She grinned. "I don't think I've ever seen you this nervous before."

I sighed. "Yeah, there's a reason for that. I mean, today's the biggest performance of my life—my wedding day."

"Oh honey, you're going to be just fine," my mother's reassuring voice said from behind me. When I glanced into the mirror, she appeared behind me. "I can't believe it's really happening. My baby is getting married." Tears glistened in her eyes, causing her to wave her hand in front of her face. "No, no, today is a happy day. No tears," she said to herself.

"I agree. Plus, I don't want to have to redo your makeup," Marion said with a smile.

Leaning over me, Mom thrust a granola bar, along with a Coke, into my hands. "You need to eat that, sweetheart. We don't want your blood sugar acting up on today of all days."

Even though I was too nervous to be hungry, I appeased my mother by unwrapping the granola bar and taking a bite. As I chewed, I couldn't help the smile that formed on my lips. The day I had met Jake my hypoglycemia had reared its head. How could I ever forget passing out right after seeing AJ, Brayden, and Rhys and realizing I wasn't on my brothers' bus? Of course, it was the moment preceding that when I had found myself in Jake's bed that meant the most. Our worlds had collided in that moment, and neither one of us would ever be the same again.

Once I finished eating, I took slow sips from the Coke out of a straw. Marion checked my lips to make sure I hadn't smudged the liner or color while eating. "Okay, makeup is done. Now for the dress and veil."

I eased up from the chair and came to stand in the middle of the room. My mom and Mia brought the dress out of the closet and then out of its massive bag. It was satin and strapless with a heavily beaded bodice. It fell into yards of satin. It was a little impractical for a beach wedding, but I didn't care. The moment I had seen it, I knew it was the dress of my dreams. I took off my robe, leaving me in a bustier and underwear.

Once I stepped into the dress, Mom went about zipping up the back. I loved the fact that a row of intricate buttons covered the zipper and gave the effect that I had been buttoned in. Jake would probably freak when he saw it, thinking he had to undo all the buttons to get me naked. I laughed at the thought.

After I was secured into the dress, I realized it was going to be tough breathing for the rest of the day between the bustier and the tight bodice. "Oomph," I muttered, as I smoothed my hand over my chest.

"Little snug, huh?" Mom asked behind me.

"Yep, just a bit. I probably overdid it last night at dinner."

Mom laughed. "I don't think so, sweetheart. They altered it to fit that way, remember?

"I guess."

"You'll get used to it."

I grinned. "I hope so, or I'm going to pass out before the day is over."

"I don't think I breathed the entire day of my wedding," Lily mused, as she fluffed out the bottom of my dress.

I shook my head. "What we sacrifice for beauty."

"Now for the veil," Marion said, as she lifted it out of the box.

The intricate lace was interwoven with pearls and sequins. It fell to the floor where it intermingled with my long train. It was held in place by a glittering tiara—an heirloom piece that I had actually rented from Tiffany's. I considered it my "something old" and "something borrowed". My something "old" also came in the form of Susan's pearls, which Jake was thrilled I was going to be wearing, and my new was everything from the dress to my underwear.

After she fixed the tiara on the top of my head, Marion stepped back and smiled. "You're ready now."

Turning left and right in front of the mirror, I took in my reflection. I blinked furiously as I tried processing what I was seeing. "Wow, I'm really standing here in my wedding dress about to get married, huh?"

Marion had worked quite a transformation with my makeup. It was softer than she usually did it for the shows, but it was also dramatic enough to bring out my eyes and highlight the peaches and cream complexion I'd been blessed to inherit. My hair, which was pulled back on the sides with sparkly combs, hung in curly waves down my back.

"You look…" my mother's voice choked off. Tears once again filled her eyes, and she bit her lip.

"Just like an angel," Mia finished with a smile.

"Which will make Jake so very happy," Lily added.

Mom nodded. "Yes, you do look absolutely angelic, sweetheart." She drew me into her arms to hug me tight. "I can't believe you're all grown up. It seems like just yesterday you were a baby in my arms."

Instead of telling my mother to stop with the over the top emotions, I just hugged her back. I knew that after today, everything would change between us. I would always be her little girl, but I was going to be Jake's wife. Someday in the future, I would be starting my own family. "I love you, Mom," I said, as I squeezed her.

"I love you, too." When she pulled away, she smiled. "No matter what, I'm so very happy for you. To love and be loved is one of the greatest miracles in life. You're truly blessed."

I smiled. "I believe I am."

After smoothing her hand over her pale pink suit, she nodded. "Well then, I think it's time we got you married."

Allison appeared with my bouquet. I brought the fragrant mixture of pink roses and white lilies to my nose. The blush-colored flowers brought out the deep pink hues of the bridesmaids' dresses while the stark white lilies were in memory of Susan, Jake's mother. Her favorite flowers had been lilies.

I drew in a deep breath and then made my way out of the bedroom. Mia and Lily trailed behind me making sure my train didn't get caught. When we got out onto the porch, I could hear the strains of the string quartet playing the pre-ceremony music. Mom hugged me one last time before she went on to be escorted to her seat by Eli and Gabe.

Glancing down below me, I saw my father. At the bottom of the stairs, he paced around on the landing. Outfitted in his best suit, he looked so handsome. But the sadness on his face was palpable, and my chest caved with pain. I knew he hadn't taken the news of my engagement well, and I guess he had hoped we'd have an even longer engagement than we had. I was his only little girl, his baby, and I imagined he felt like Jake was stealing me away. At the same time, he had always treated Jake with love and respect, and I was so thankful for that.

The moment he saw me, he forced a smile to his lips. "There she is. The beautiful bride," he said.

Clutching my enormous bouquet, I carefully made my way down the narrow, stone stairs. When I finally reached him, he pulled me into his arms and gave me a tight squeeze. "You look absolutely breathtaking, sweetheart."

"Thank you, Daddy." I pulled away to smile at him. "Ready to give me away?"

He shook his head. "I could never do that. I may walk you down that aisle and consent for Jake to marry you, but I'll never fully give you away. You'll always be my little girl." His hand came to his chest. "You'll forever remain right in my heart, Abigail."

"Oh Daddy," I murmured, as tears stung my eyes. When I glanced back at the girls, I expected them to chide me on crying and potentially wrecking my makeup. Instead, their eyes were shiny with tears as well.

"So sweet," Mia murmured, as she quickly wiped her eyes. From her expression, I knew she was thinking of how hard it was going to be for her own father at her wedding in a few months.

The wedding coordinator appeared wearing a headset and carrying a clipboard. "Okay, I need the flower girl and ring bearer to line up followed by the bridesmaids."

After handing her bouquet to Mia, Lily bent down to straighten Jude's shirt and tie. "You know what to do, right?"

I could tell he was fighting the urge to roll his eyes at her. "Yes, Mommy. I walk down the aisle holding the pillow, and then stand next to Daddy. I'm not a baby, you know."

With a smile, Lily patted his chest. "I know, sweetheart. I just wanted to check." She then turned her attention to Melody. After she fluffed out Melody's frilly dress and adjusted her headband, Lily asked, "And what about you, Miss Priss? Do you know what to do?"

"Throw the flowers!" she cried with a grin.

I laughed at her enthusiasm while Lily shook her head. "No, you're not supposed to throw the petals. You need to gently toss them on the sand. Do it just like we practiced. Okay?"

Melody bobbed her head, but in my mind, I didn't think she was totally onboard with the whole "gentle" thing. Lily rose up to give me a tight smile. "Don't worry. I'll be right behind her in case she goes crazy or something."

"It'll be fine," I reassured her.

The wedding coordinator motioned for Jude and Melody. Just as they started around the chairs toward the aisle, the string ensemble started playing *Ave Maria*. As Jude and Melody started down the aisle, Lily followed close behind them. Then Mia went followed by Allison, who I had asked to be my maid of honor. There were friends in my past I could have asked, but Allison was about to become my sister-in-law. It felt like the right thing to do. And regardless of how Jake felt about his father, he truly loved his little sister with all his heart.

"Okay, Abby, it's time."

Unable to form words, I merely nodded. My arm trembled slightly as I slipped it through my father's. "I've got you, sweetheart," he said, as he smiled down at me. The quartet changed music, and the sound of *Here Comes the Bride* filled the air. This was really it—the moment I became Jake's wife.

As the crowd rose from their chairs, I put one barefoot in front of the other. Craning my neck, I desperately tried to catch a glimpse of Jake. I could see Brayden, AJ, and Rhys in their island casual khaki pants, crisp white, button-down shirts, and pink vests. But there was no Jake. Finally, as we curved around the last row of chairs to start up the aisle, my eyes met his. The smile that spread across his lips caused my heart to still and restart.

I couldn't remember a time when he had looked more handsome. His dark hair was perfectly slicked back. His vest hugged his muscular frame while his biceps bulged against the fabric of his shirt. Even from my place down the aisle, I could see his deep blue eyes sparkling in the twilight. I couldn't believe how lucky I was to be marrying this gorgeous man. But it wasn't what he looked like on the outside that mattered to me. It was his caring heart and sensitive soul that made the true attraction for me.

My mind was on sensory overload as I tried to take in every detail of my walk down the aisle. The smiling faces of friends and family, the gentle breeze that rippled through my hair, the way the warm sand squished between my toes, the sound of the waves crashing against the shore below us.

When I reached Jake's side, the sun had started its descent into the west, sending an array of reds and oranges across the deep, blue sky. In the fading sunlight, thousands of candles and twinkling lights lit our perfect piece of heaven on the shore.

Kissing my cheek, my dad then left my side to take his place at the head of the altar. He was pulling double duty giving me away, as well as performing the ceremony. "Dearly beloved, we're gathered here in the sight of God to join together this man and this woman in the bonds of holy matrimony…"

I couldn't help tuning my dad out to glance over at Jake. I was rewarded with a pleased grin from him. Leaning over slightly, he whispered, "Oh Abby, you look like a dream…like my true angel."

Gazing up at him, I mouthed, "Thank you."

When my dad cleared his throat, both Jake and I jumped and then quickly gave him our full attention. "It's normally at this part of the ceremony when I ask who gives the woman in marriage. Of course, I already know the answer to this question." Smiling at Jake, my dad said, "Laura, and I, along with her brothers, proudly and happily give Abby's hand to you, Jake."

"I gladly take it, sir," Jake replied, with a grin.

"You know, from the time Abby was born, Laura and I prayed that God would send her a companion. Someone she could spend her life in love with. Someone to support her in the good times and bad and be her true soul mate. Of course, we didn't expect him to come in the package of a tattooed rock star."

Laughter echoed around us. When it had faded away, my dad's expression sobered. "Two years ago when I first met you, Jake, I don't think I could have ever fathomed being in this place today. I wanted Abby to marry someday—one day long, long in the future. But our time isn't always divine, and I have no doubts that you two are meant to start your lives together at *this* very moment in time."

"Thank you, sir," Jake said softly.

Dad nodded at my brothers and Micah. Jake and I had argued over what song to have played at the ceremony. Finally, after months of discussion, we finally decided on *God Bless the Broken Road*. As Micah began singing the familiar lyrics, Jake took my hands in his. He squeezed them tight before giving me a beaming smile. As my brothers' voices harmonized, Jake's thumbs rubbed circles over the back of my hand. Not once did he take his eyes from mine.

When the song faded to a close, my dad opened his Bible to begin the vows. "Jake, repeat after me," he instructed.

Jake nodded and turned his attention away from my father and back to me. "I, Jacob Ethan Slater, take you Abigail Elizabeth Renard to be my lawfully wedded wife…" As he started to echo the words my father said, he blinked back the tears. Considering how Jake was usually so cocky and so sure of himself, his vulnerability broke me completely.

When it became my turn, I could barely contain my sobs as I repeated my vows. I was a shaking, stuttering mess, but somehow I made it through them. "Love you," Jake mouthed with a smile.

"Love you more," I replied.

"And now, for the giving and receiving of rings," my father said.

I turned to Allison while Jake turned to AJ. "With this ring, I thee wed," I murmured as I slid the platinum band on Jake's left hand. After Jake slid mine on, we turned to my dad.

"By the power vested in me by God's holy ordinance and the state of Texas, I now pronounce you husband and wife." With a little less bravado, he glanced at Jake and added, "You may now kiss the bride."

A smile curved on Jake's lips as his hands came to cup my face. Tenderly his thumbs stroked my cheeks before he leaned in to kiss me. While our lips lingered together, Jake dropped his hands to then wrap me in his arms. He squeezed me tight against him. When he pulled away, tears shimmered in his eyes. "I love you, Mrs. Slater," Jake whispered into my ear.

No matter how many times he said the words, I simply couldn't grow tired of them. I knew I wouldn't for the rest of my life. "I love you, too. So, so much," I replied.

My father's booming voice cut us off. "I'm happy to present Mr. and Mrs. Jake Slater!"

Applause cut through the air as everyone rose out of the chairs. The quartet struck up the *Bridal March* as I took my bouquet back from Allison. With my cheeks stinging from smiling so broadly, I slipped my arm through Jake's, and we started down the aisle as man and wife. As corny as it sounds, it felt just like I was walking on air. I couldn't remember a time when I had felt such joy, such love, and such contentment.

After an evening filled with dinner and dancing, I stood on the dock with Abby as we waved goodbye to the last of our wedding party. With one arm wrapped securely around Abby's waist, she snuggled tighter against my side. We watched the lights of the catamaran get further and further away. Finally, we were alone. Just us. With an entire island all to ourselves.

Gazing down at her, I smiled. "Man, I thought they'd never leave."

She giggled. "I know. I thought we were going to just have to go up to the house and leave them all down here."

"The sad fact is it's only midnight."

Abby's brows shot up in surprise. "Seriously? I thought it was at least three am."

I laughed. "No, the last boat for the shore leaves at midnight. If we hadn't got their asses on there, we would have had a full house for our honeymoon."

Abby's nose wrinkled. "That would have been a nightmare."

"Anxious to have me all to yourself, huh?"

"Mmm, hmm," she replied before yawning.

"Are you tired, Mrs. Slater?"

"Just a little," she admitted sheepishly.

"I kept you up too late last night."

She shook her head. "I don't regret one moment of *that*."

"That's my girl." Leaning over, I cupped my arms beneath her knees and swept her off her feet.

Her eyes widened. "Jake, what are you doing?" she demanded.

"You said you were tired, so I'm going to carry you back to the house like a good husband."

Abby snorted as I started trudging across the cold, wet sand. "This is really chivalrous of you, but you're going to strain yourself."

I cut my eyes over to hers. "Are you insinuating that I'm not manly enough to carry you across this beach?"

"Come on, Jake. This is silly. Put me down."

"All right. Fine. But don't try to say later on that I never did anything romantic for you." With her still in my arms, I sank to my knees. She squealed when I pitched her forward onto the sand.

"What are—?"

With a shrug, I replied, "You wanted me to put you down, so I was just obliging you."

She glared up at me in the moonlight. "Now I have a wet and cold ass, thanks to you."

"Hmm, we can't have that now, can we?" Looming over her, I nudged her onto her back, which was what I had planned on when I let her down. "Let me warm you up." I leaned in to bring my lips to hers when someone cleared her throat above me. Glancing up from Abby, I saw the wedding coordinator smiling apologetically at me. "Yes?"

"I just wanted to let you know that everything is ready for you at the house. It should only be another thirty minutes for the catering crew to break everything down. Then you'll have the island to yourselves."

"Thank you."

With a curt nod, she turned and started high tailing it away from us. "Glad she's gone. Now where were we?"

"The part where you get off me, so we can go to the house and have our well-needed privacy?"

I groaned. "No, not that part. I wanted the part where I made love to you in the moonlight with the waves crashing over us."

Abby laughed. "That sounds wonderful, but not when we have a potential audience. You can take me in a hundred different ways all over this beach tomorrow when we're alone."

"Damn, is that a promise?"

"Yes, it is."

"Hmm, okay then." In a fluid motion, I rose to my feet and then extended my hand to her. When she slipped hers inside mine, I pulled her off the sand. Keeping her hand in mine, we started walking up the beach to the house.

As we went by the bustling caters, they kept their heads down and tried to be invisible to us. "Thank you all, again. Everything was just wonderful," Abby gushed.

A few "You're Welcomes" were said while they kept working. "You're too sweet for your own good, you know that?" I asked, as we walked up the stairs.

"It doesn't hurt to say thank you and show your gratitude for a good job," Abby countered.

"A lot of people wouldn't. You've never let your stardom or fame go to your head. It's just one of the million things I love about you."

"I'll be sure to say thank you for the amazing orgasms you're going to give me tonight," she said, with a little smirk.

My brows rose as I thought about her cocky little response. She was betting on some orgasms, and I sure as hell intended on giving them to her. "Oh, you're going to pay for that one, Miss Sassy," I said, reaching out for her. She squealed and ran ahead of me into the house. When I caught up with her, I started to grab her but then stopped. She stood stock still in the middle of the living room. With her back to me, she stared straight ahead. I knew she was taking in the flickering candles and rose petals that led down the hallway.

Abby glanced over her shoulder at me, her blue eyes wide with surprise. "You had them do this?"

I shrugged. "I made a few suggestions to their 'romance package'."

"It's beautiful," she murmured, with a small smile. Gathering up the front of her dress, she began padding barefoot down the hallway. With the candlelight illuminating her golden hair and skin, she looked just like an angel. My angel—for now and always. Fuck, how did an asshole like me ever get so lucky?

I heard her sharp intake of breath when she entered the master suite at the end of the hallway. "Oh Jake," she whispered. Candles lit the interior of the room while on top of the bed, red, pink, and purple rose petals were formed into a giant heart.

"You don't think it's cheesy?" I asked tentatively.

"Never." She turned around to wrap her arms around me. "The fact that it came from your heart makes it even more special."

"I wanted to make tonight beautiful for you. I know chicks dig shit like flowers and candles."

Abby smiled. "It is wonderful, Jake, but you're all I need to make this night wonderful. You and your love."

"Mmm, I like hearing you say that," I said, before leaning in to kiss her. As her ready mouth worked against mine, I knew how hard it was going to be to reign myself in tonight. But more than anything, I was ready to get the show on the road. When I pulled away, I stared into her expectant eyes. "Turn around," I commanded.

Abby quickly obliged. Her hands came to sweep up the long stands of her hair to give me better access to undress her. When I caught sight of the long row of fine pearl buttons, I sucked in a harsh breath of frustration. "Fuck me! Are you serious?"

She burst out laughing. "It's just a zipper, babe."

"Thank God," I muttered. My fingers went to the middle of her back to find the zipper. I tugged it down. Once the dress bowed open, I leaned forward to bestow a trail of tender kisses across the exposed skin of her shoulder blades. I was rewarded with a dreamy little sigh from Abby as she arched her back toward me. After I'd given enough attention to the soft, creamy skin on her back and the base of her spine, my hands then went to the top of the dress to push it off her shoulders.

All I could see on Abby was a white, lacy push up bra thing that extended down her back to her waist. I could only imagine how perfect she looked from the front with her tits all pushed up, just waiting for me to touch and suck on them. Just the thought sent my dick pounding against the zipper of my pants.

I slid the dress off her hips and let it drop to the floor. Offering my hand, I helped Abby step out of it. "Mmm," I murmured, as she stood before me in only a lacy, white thong and the bra thing that sure as hell did thrust her tits up into my face. A thousand and one different scenarios entered my head of fucking her fast and hard until we were a sweaty mess and she was screaming my name.

"You look like you're about to devour me," she whispered, her cheeks flushing in the candlelight.

"I want to—I really do. But more than anything, I want to make love you as your husband tonight."

"Oh, yes," she gasped.

I took her hands in mine and then brought them to my vest. Abby made quick work of unbuttoning me. She tossed the vest to the floor and then went to work on my shirt. To help things along, I unbuttoned and unzipped my pants. When I was only in my boxer shorts, I gripped her waist and pushed her back to the bed. "Lie down," I said.

Without taking her eyes off mine, she eased on top of the heart made out of rose petals on the bed. I knelt down on the mattress. As I loomed over her, I couldn't help being amazed at how beautiful she was. How in the world a bastard like me had been gifted this angel of perfection I would never know. She would always be too good for me—too sweet, too pure, too giving of herself.

"Hey, what's wrong?" Abby asked, her hand coming up to cup my cheek.

"Nothing."

"Jake?" she implored.

I sighed raggedly. "I was just thinking how much I don't deserve you."

Her tender fingers rubbed my cheek. "Oh no, baby. That's not true at all."

With a smile, I realized her love for me would always blind her of my faults. Her sweet words fueled me on. I kissed and licked across her collarbone, leaving little love bites as I went. My hands came to the clasps on the front of the bra, and I popped them open one by one. Her breasts sprang free and into my ready mouth. I sucked hard on one pink nipple. After increasing the pressure, I pulled back to let my tongue flick across it. As it hardened beneath me, I let it fall free of my mouth before blowing across the puckered tip.

"Jake," Abby moaned, her legs scissoring beneath us.

"Patience, Angel." I understood her frustration. My dick pounded against the front of my boxer shorts to get free and be buried deep inside her. But this was a once in a lifetime deal—the very reason why she had wanted to abstain. Tonight was supposed to be special, amazing, and heartfelt, and by God, I was going to make sure it was.

I licked a wet trail from the valley between her breasts down to her abdomen. My fingers came to grip the sides of her thong before I slid it down over her legs. She opened wide, giving me a great view of her pussy, but I wasn't quite ready for that. Instead, I rolled her over so she was on her stomach. Starting at her feet, I kissed and licked up her calves to her thighs. Then I alternated with the other leg. Little goose bumps puckered her flesh, as my mouth warmed over them. Abby's fingers gripped the sheets as she writhed beneath me. Her little whimpers told me I was doing everything right to extend her pleasure as long as I could.

When I got to her ass, I pushed her up on her knees. I kissed and licked each delicious globe before I thrust my tongue between her legs. Abby cried out and jerked her hips back against me. After I spread her apart with my fingers, I continued licking and sucking her clit. It only took a few minutes before she came against my tongue. As she was coming down, I dared to slide my tongue backwards from her slit, which caused Abby to freeze. "You okay, Angel?" My voice vibrated against her ass.

"Y-Yes, but..."

"But what?"

"You've never done that."

"Do you not want me to?"

She remained silent. "No, it's okay," she whispered.

I laughed. "So you liked it then?"

Glancing over her shoulder at me, she smiled. "Yes, but don't be getting any ideas about putting anything else there."

"You know, I'll take whatever you give me." Before she could protest that she never wanted to deny me satisfaction, I let my tongue circle the puckered hole once more. When she shuddered, I decided to go easy on her and bring my tongue back to her clit. Abby surprised me by twisting around and coming up on her hands and knees in front of me.

"It's your turn now," she said, before tugging the waistband of my boxer shorts down.

"I wanted it to be about you tonight."

Abby shook her head. "But I want to give my new husband some pleasure."

"And you will the moment I get buried deep inside you."

Her brows crinkled as she stared up at me. "Are you sure?"

My hand came to cup her cheek. "Yeah, baby. I'm sure."

After I kicked out of my boxer shorts, I eased Abby onto her back. Her legs widened to allow me between them. I kissed her eyelids, the tip of her nose, and her cheeks. "I love you," I murmured, holding her face in my hands.

She smiled up at me with such raw emotion shining in her eyes that my chest clenched. "I love you, too, Jake. For now and always."

With Abby's sweet words surrounding me, I thrust inside her. My eyes locked on hers as I kept my movements tediously slow at first. Abby's fingertips swept up and down my back. I thought of the times her nails had dug into the skin during some hardcore fucking. But there was no place for that tonight. We were making love together as man and wife for the first time. And it was the most fucking amazing sexual experience I could ever hope for.

We rarely came at the same time, but tonight we did. We were one body and one soul. And I thanked God, and all my lucky stars, that Abby was mine.

Chapter Six
"Abby"

Curly wisps of smoke billowed into the night's sky from the enormous bonfire on the beach. As the heat from the crackling flames warmed me from head to toe, I snuggled my naked body closer to Jake's side. The moment felt so good that I couldn't help sighing with absolute contentment. "This is wonderful, isn't it?"

"Oh yeah. It would feel just like we were home if it weren't for the sand in my ass crack."

I giggled as I raised my head to look into his eyes that were twinkling with amusement. "It was your idea to have sex all over this beach, remember?"

"Oh yes, I remember every fuckable detail," he replied, before nipping my lips.

True to his word, Jake had taken me in almost every position possible out on the beach. After breakfast, a quick dip in the ocean had led to an almost exact recreation of the beach scene in *From Here to Eternity*. We made it a little further onto the shore before the palms of my hands got extremely exfoliated after he'd pushed me onto my knees and had taken me doggy style. I never knew there could be such a thing as sand burn, but I had red, almost raw places on my elbows and knees.

Around six, the catamaran had arrived with dinner. We ate outside on the porch and watched the gorgeous sunset. To walk off the enormous amount of food we had consumed, we took a stroll on the beach that led to another roll in the sand. Once we recovered, Jake had lit the bonfire before grabbing a blanket and wrapping me in his arms. The conversation flowed easily between us as we rehashed all that had happened at the wedding and reception.

"Jude and Melody did so well, didn't they?" I asked.

Jake nodded. "They sure did. I think they'll have their duties down to an art by the time AJ and Mia's wedding rolls around."

"Probably so. Of course, Mia wants Bella to have a part, too." I smiled up at him. "Didn't Bella look adorable yesterday? I loved when you danced with her and Melody together. So sweet."

Jake remained uncharacteristically quiet. "You and Bella together are trouble."

My brows furrowed at his comment. "What do you mean?"

"It was the way you looked at her while you held her."

"And just how did I look at her?"

"Like you were dreaming she was yours."

"I did not!" I protested, as embarrassed heat enflamed my cheeks.

"Yeah, you did."

I stared up at the sky encrusted with glittering stars. There was some truth in what Jake said. As Bella snuggled into my chest, emitting a tiny little sigh, I did imagine what it would be like to have a baby—Jake's baby—sleeping in my arms. "I was just holding her for Mia and AJ to dance," I said softly.

"But you did wish she was yours," Jake insisted.

"*Ours*," I corrected him. I heaved a frustrated sigh. "She's my goddaughter—I'm always going to feel a close connection to her. But I know she has two amazing parents who love her. And yeah, I was thinking about babies and children when I held her. Mainly, it was the overwhelming emotion of just how much I want a baby of our own—not just mine, but yours." I cut my eyes over to his. "I don't have to dream or fantasize about what will really happen in the future, do I?"

Jake jerked a hand through his hair. "I've been worried when you became Mrs. Jake Slater, your desire for kids would go into overdrive, and now I see I was right."

"Is wanting a baby such a bad thing?"

"When it's going to be five years before we have one, then yeah, it is bad for you to get so attached to the idea."

My brows shot up in surprise. "Now it's five years? I thought it was two US tours and one world?"

Jake shrugged. "It's just a good number."

Peering into his face, I asked, "Why are you really afraid of having kids?"

"I'm not."

"Yes, you are."

Jake's jaw clenched and unclenched before he spoke. "Look, I'll openly admit I'm a selfish son of a bitch about having kids right now, but I'm *not* afraid. You're only twenty-three, Abby. You have the rest of your life to be tied down with a kid."

My mouth gaped open at his words. "*Tied down*? Is that what you think of Mia or Lily? Are they bound by their kids?"

"No, that's not what I meant."

"Then what do you mean?"

With a grimace, Jake said, "Kids change everything, okay? We've only had two years together. I want a few more before we bring kids into the picture."

"Is your aversion to fatherhood because of your dad?"

Jake's expression darkened. "What the fuck is that supposed to mean?"

I opened my mouth and then closed it shut. I didn't think I was ready to test out my theory on Jake, especially now that he was pissed off. "Abby?" he prompted.

Drawing in a ragged breath, I exhaled it before I responded. "I think you're afraid that when you have the pressures of a wife and kids, you'll become your father and stray." Feeling more courageous, I continued on. "Somehow, you think if we don't have kids for a long time, you can prolong what you feel is the inevitable—that you will cheat on me and lose me."

His mouth fell open my summation, and I knew then that I had hit the nail on the head. "You're not your father, Jake," I said in a whisper.

"I know that," he snapped.

"Then don't be afraid of making his mistakes."

He threw up his hands in frustration. "This is bullshit."

Staring down at the checked blanket, I said in a low voice, "By the way you're reacting, I think you and I both know it's true. But regardless of all the shit with your dad, you have to know that your mother never, ever felt tied down by you. She was grateful for every moment she had with you."

"Do *not* bring my mother into this conversation," he growled.

"I'm sorry."

"You know what really worries me? That you'll decide when it's time for us to have kids, whether I'm ready or not."

"And how exactly would I do that?"

His blue eyes flashed. "By suddenly forgetting to take your birth control."

I gasped. "You think I would actually go so far as to go behind your back to conceive a child?"

"If I kept denying you, then yes, I do think you would do that."

"Y-You're…an asshole!" I shouted before I clambered to my feet. Wrapping my arms around my naked chest, I stalked away from the bonfire toward the house. Halfway across the sand, the anger began to fade, and hot tears streamed down my cheeks. Craning my neck over my shoulder, I hoped that Jake was coming after to me to apologize or talk things out. Unfortunately, he remained at the fire pit.

I couldn't believe the things he had said—the way he felt about me somehow deceiving him and getting pregnant. It wounded me deep to my core that he would ever think I could do such a thing. Our relationship had always been built on trust, and now he was making me question that. There was also the fact that he had confirmed my fears about him being like his father and cheating. Deep down, I never could believe he would ever do such a thing, but now the doubt was planted in my mind, and it caused my chest to ache.

When I got inside the house, I was mentally and physically exhausted. But just the thought of getting into the bed where we'd consummated our marriage and made love the night before was too painful. Instead, I threw on a pair of shorts and a T-shirt before collapsing onto the couch. I wrapped myself in a cocoon of blankets. It didn't take long for the tears to come again. Never did I think I would spend one night of my honeymoon crying myself to sleep, but it looked like that was going to happen tonight. I brought my hands to my face and started sobbing uncontrollably.

I don't know how long I spent sitting out beside the bonfire. I was too raw from my fight with Abby to go after her right away. I knew I needed to apologize. The hard part was that both of us had spoken the truth. Abby had all too easily guessed my issues with fatherhood, and I had let my worst fears about her slip out. In the two years we'd been together, we'd rarely fought over anything of real importance. I'm not saying I didn't treat her like a callous dickhead several times when we first started dating, but everything else had always clicked into place so easily for us. Now we were twenty-four hours into our marriage and had just experienced our first major fight. And it was a real doozy.

Some newlyweds fought about paint colors and finances. Abby and I had to go straight for the jugular and fight about our future family. With a ragged sigh, I rubbed my eyes that were stinging from the bonfire's smoke. At least I thought it was the smoke. Maybe I was being a real pussy and crying over our fight.

The truth was I didn't hate the idea of having kids someday— just not anytime soon. I loved Jude and Melody, and now Bella had me wrapped around her little finger. But at the end of playtime or hanging out with them, they went home with their parents. They weren't my sole responsibility. Babies and kids took a lot of work, time, and energy that I wasn't ready to give yet. Of course, I wanted to get Abby pregnant someday. She was going to make the most amazing mother in the entire world. But I didn't know why she had to have such baby fever now when she was only twenty-three. She was acting like she was thirty-five, and her biological clock was ticking. We shared so many of the same likes, dreams, and passions that it was hard imagining we were so far off the mark with the baby thing.

After extinguishing the fire, I dejectedly made my way to the house. I didn't know what I was going to say to Abby. I tried going over it in my mind as I trudged through the cool sand. Somehow I knew I needed to lead off with *Yes, I'm a giant, unfeeling bastard*…and then follow up with *Please, please forgive me.* At the same time, I knew I had to somehow make it clear that although I was sorry for what I said, I wasn't changing my mind about when we were going to start a family.

The house was dark when I got inside. I started for the bedroom when I heard a sniffle from the living room. Glancing over my shoulder, I saw a heap of blankets on the couch. Somewhere underneath it was Abby. And she was crying.

Damn, I was a bastard.

With an exasperated sigh, I threw my head back and gazed up at the ceiling. This is so not how I envisioned this night to be. "Abby, you don't need to sleep on the couch. If anyone should, it's me."

"I'm fine," she sniffed.

"Would you please come to bed, so we can talk about this?" She huffed contemptuously like I was some mega horndog, trying to get her into bed to screw through my apology. "I mean, I think the mattress is big enough that you don't have to worry about touching me if you don't want to."

"Just leave me alone," she snapped.

Although the words "I'm so sorry" formed on my tongue, I couldn't say them. Instead, I grumbled, "Whatever," before stalking back to the bedroom. I jerked the sheet and comforter down before flopping down on the mattress. The instant I turned over, pain jackknifed through my chest. Although I was all alone in bed, Abby remained all around me. Her scent of jasmine and vanilla mingled on the sheets while her strawberry shampoo filled the pillow next to me. A few withered rose petals still littered the sheets from where we had made love last night.

I don't know why I remained in bed instead of going to apologize. Oh yeah, I was being my usual stubborn-asshole self. But although it had come out all wrong, my words were steeped in truth. I wasn't ready to be a father, and my greatest fear was Abby becoming pregnant by accident or on the sly. Deep down, I couldn't imagine that she would ever do something like that, but it was still a fear.

After tossing and turning for a couple of hours, I finally fell into a restless asleep.

When I woke up the next morning, I rolled over to snuggle against Abby. The moment I felt the cold, empty spot, it came back to me what had happened the night before. "Fuck," I muttered, as I rubbed the sleep out of my eyes. If I didn't man up and apologize, the remaining five days of our island paradise were going to be absolute hell.

I slipped out of bed and slid into my boxer shorts and then made a quick bathroom stop. "Abby?" I called from the bedroom. "Angel, we need to talk."

After she didn't respond, I stalked down the hall and to the living room. Gazing around, I found the room empty. Craning my neck, I peered into the kitchen. She wasn't there either. After I'd checked the spare bathroom and bedroom, fear streaked through my chest that she'd called the shore and asked for the boat. I ran outside onto the porch. I started for the stairs when a flash of red out in the water caught my eye. Gazing out into the water, I saw her swimming in my favorite bikini of hers.

With a sigh, I made my way off the porch and down the beach. She had just surfaced again when I started into the water. At the sight of me, her eyes widened and then she quickly looked away. I thought for a minute she might try to swim away, but instead, she held her ground. "Hey," I said, when I finally reached her.

"Hey," she replied softly, still refusing to look me in the eye.

"Angel...I need you to look at me. Please." When she finally lifted her chin and met my gaze, I sighed. "I'm so sorry for the things I said last night."

Her eyes closed as if she were in pain. Finally, she opened them. "I'm sorry, too."

My brows furrowed. Here we were both apologizing, yet there still was this giant divide between us. As I literally treaded water, I felt like I was fighting to keep my head above the surface in our relationship. How did we get back to the way we were?

"I guess this was our first fight as a married couple, huh?" I asked.

"A pretty big one, too," she murmured.

"I'm sorry. I hate fighting with you, Angel. Most of all, I hate to see you upset."

Abby's blue eyes blazed with intensity. "Then try not to say such hurtful things next time."

"I'll try. I promise."

"Okay."

As an uncomfortable silence still hung around us, I sighed. "You know, I was afraid when I woke up and found the house empty that you'd left me."

"I would never do that to you."

"I know. It was just this irrational fear I had." I exhaled a long, ragged breath. "I guess, it's kinda like the fear I have of you getting pregnant on the sly."

Abby shook her head. "How could you think I would ever do that?"

I furiously rubbed my face, letting the salty water sting my eyes. "I don't know why." At her wounded expression, I added, "I don't think, deep down, that you would really do that, but, it is a fear of mine.'"

She inched a little closer to me. "We're in this marriage together, Jake. It's a partnership where we make our decisions together. Even though I would love nothing more than to have your baby, I don't want to until you're ready. More than anything, I want to know that you trust me."

"I'm sorry, Angel. I do trust you. I swear. You've never been anything but trustworthy and faithful to me."

"Then stop worrying."

I drew in a ragged breath. "Somehow I can't help but wonder how you can still love me when I'm denying you this."

"Oh Jake, my love for you doesn't stop just because there's a rough patch in the road, or I don't get what I want."

"Really?" It was hard for me to wrap my mind around the fact that someone could sacrifice so much for me just because they loved me.

She nodded emphatically. "Of course not. I may be disappointed or hurt, but I could never love you less."

I stared into her eyes, seeing the unconditional love for me burning bright in them. I felt like such a fool for ever doubting her. "Angel, I love you so much," I blurted before jerking her into my arms. The motion caused us to lose our balance, and we dipped under the surface of the water. We remained lip-locked with our arms wrapped around each other as our feet kicked to keep us from sinking. When we broke the surface again, I pulled away. "Let's get to where we can touch."

"Okay," Abby murmured, her blue eyes hooded.

We swam closer to the shore, and the moment our feet could touch again, I took her back in my arms. Abby gripped my shoulders before hopping up to wrap her legs around my waist. My fingers went to the strings at her back. With one tug, the bikini top gave way, and her delicious tits spilled out. Gripping her hips, I pushed her further up my body where I could suck on her nipples. As they puckered and hardened in my mouth, Abby gasped. Her fingers came to tangle through the wet strands of my hair. "Jake," she moaned.

"I want to fuck you, Angel," I growled against her chest.

"Not here," she panted.

"No love-making in the ocean?" I questioned as I ground my erection against her core.

Her hooded eyes met mine, and she gave me a lazy smile. "It's not good for the girl."

"Oh, really?"

She shook her head. "You'd be good, but the potential infections from the salt water wouldn't."

I laughed. "Okay, Angel, I'll take you to the house."

With her legs wrapped tight around my waist and my arms underneath her ass, I started walking us out of the water. I kept my mouth firmly on Abby's. Anxious to be inside her, my tongue thrust in and out of her deliciously warm mouth just like I wanted my dick to be doing. At the same time, Abby kept up a relentless pace of rubbing herself against my dick.

We'd only made it half-way up the beach when she broke our intense kiss. "Take me out here, Jake," she insisted.

My brows shot up in surprise. "You can't wait for the house?"

"No," she moaned. "I want you right now."

"Damn, Angel, are you trying to kill me?"

"Please," she begged.

Gazing at the palm trees below the house, I steered us over to them. I eased her down onto her feet on the sand before ripping her bikini bottoms down. I couldn't resist bringing my mouth between her legs. When my tongue flicked against her clit, Abby cried out, and her knees buckled. With one arm, I pushed her back upright. Her fingers tugged on the strands of my hair as I licked and sucked her pussy. I didn't bother thrusting my tongue into her. No, I was reserving that one for my throbbing dick.

Just as she was about to come, I pulled away. She whimpered in protest and thrust her hips forward. "You're going to have to wait until I'm inside you," I said, as I rose up off the sand.

"No fair," she pouted.

"Well, I could say you've been a bad girl—you know, refusing to talk to me last night and making me think you'd left me on the island."

"I'm sorry."

"So you admit you were a bad girl?"

She eyed me for a moment, trying to decide how playing along with me would benefit her. "Yes, I guess I was a little bad." After nibbling on her bottom lip for a moment, she floored the hell out of me by saying, "Maybe you should spank me and teach me a lesson."

At just the suggestion, my head snapped back like she slapped me. We'd never gotten real down and dirty like this. Sure, a playful smack here and there, but never like what she was suggesting. "You think you deserve it?"

"Mmm, hmm."

"Fine then." Grabbing her hands, I jerked them above her head. I then whirled her around and placed them on the tree trunk. For a moment, my hand massaged the globe of her ass. Glancing at me over her shoulder, Abby waited expectantly for my next move. Deciding to really play the part, I barked, "Did I say you could look at me?"

Abby jerked her gaze from mine and stared ahead. I pulled my hand away and then cracked my open palm against her cheek. She gasped as her whole body jerked. Just as she was getting used to the sensation, my hand went to her other cheek, and I smacked it good. "Do you like that?"

"Yes, I do."

"Is it making you a little wet?"

"Maybe." She glanced over her shoulder and shot me a defiant gaze. "Why don't you check and see?"

"You better hold on tight. I plan on fucking you hard."

"Good." She gripped the trunk of the tree as I made work of getting out of my boxers. "Please, Jake."

Without any more foreplay, I slammed into her with one brutal thrust. We both groaned. When I recovered enough to think more about my actions, I asked, "Did I hurt you?"

"No. And don't stop."

"My pleasure." My hands came to grip her hips so tight I hoped I didn't end up bruising her. With a relentless pace, I thrust into her while pushing her on and off my dick. The sound of wet skin slapping together, echoed around us. I leaned into to lick and bite at her neck. My teeth scraped along the sensitive skin below her ear.

"Jake, oh yes, Jake!" Abby cried, as she fought to keep her hold on the tree. It was only a few moments later when I felt her walls tense around my dick, and she went over the edge. She collapsed against the tree trunk, but I pulled her back against me so she wouldn't get scraped. After a few minutes of harsh thrusting, I came with a loud shouting curse, burying my face in the silky strands of her hair. As I started coming back to myself, I slipped my arms around her waist while nuzzling her neck.

"You okay, Angel?"

"I don't think I can walk," she admitted.

I glanced down at her sheepish expression. "Aw, come here, baby," I said. I picked her up and then gently deposited her into the hammock next to us. I grabbed her bikini bottoms off the ground next to us to do a little clean-up on her.

With a lazy grin, she said, "Aw, thanks. You're my hero."

"No, thank *you*. That was some fantastic fucking."

She giggled. "You're terrible."

"It would almost be worth another fight to have make-up sex like that, I mused as I eased in beside her.

Her eyes drooped closed, and she yawned. "No, I don't want to fight anymore," she protested feebly.

I kissed her cheek. "I know, Angel. I was just teasing you. The last thing I want to ever do again is hurt you."

She snuggled against me, draping her hip over my thigh. "I love you."

"I love you, more."

Her index finger came to trail circles over my chest. "You know, I really missed you last night."

"I missed you, too. And waking up with you."

She grinned. "So you could have your morning wood taken care of?"

I rolled my eyes. "No, so I could feel you next to me." I stared intently into her eyes. "I've never felt more safe or more content than when I'm in your arms." I stroked her cheek with my finger. "You make everything better, Angel. Hell, you make it easier to breathe."

Tears pooled in Abby's eyes before she dipped her head to kiss me, letting her love for me flow out through her actions. When she pulled away, she smiled before laying her head on my chest right above my heart.

Completely sexually satisfied and exhausted from my restless night before, I fell into a deep sleep. When Abby and I finally woke up, it was mid-afternoon. "Did you have a nice nap?" I asked her.

"Yes, because I was with you."

"You're such a sweet little flatterer," I said, as I kissed the top of her forehead.

"You're welcome."

"Hungry?" I asked.

"Mmm, hmm, but just for you," she replied, her hand coming to cup my dick.

My eyes widened in surprise. "Damn, I think I've married a nympho!"

She grinned up at me. "Would you want me any other way?"

I laughed. "No, I suppose not."

Within seconds, her hand managed to work me to full mast. "I'm not sure this is going to work," I said, motioning to the hammock and how easy it was to have a foot or arm poke through the ropes.

"Where there's a will, there's a way," she replied, with a wink. She then rolled over to straddle me. Her hips rose up, while her hand guided my erection deep inside her.

"Ready for me already, Mrs. Slater?" I panted, as my dick slid in and out of her wet core.

"I'm always ready for you," she murmured breathlessly.

"That makes me a very happy man," I replied. My hand came to cup her bouncing breasts. Abby moaned and gasped with pleasure as I pinched and tweaked her nipples to hardened buds. As our movements grew more frantic, the hammock started to jerk and sway. One hand abandoned Abby's breast to stroke between her legs. Her moans grew more and more intense the harder I stroked her clit. She then cried out and threw her head back as the first wave of the orgasm hit her. The feel of her walls tensing around me caused me to come. Once I finished shuddering inside her, I grabbed Abby's shoulders and pulled her down to me. As she rested her head on my shoulder, she remained straddling me with my dick still buried inside her.

I ran my hands over the silky strands of her hair. "That was amazing."

"I thought so too," came her muffled reply against my chest.

When I opened my mouth to say something else, the rumbling of Abby's stomach made me smile. "Guess we worked up an appetite, huh?"

She pulled her head up to smile sheepishly at me. "I didn't have breakfast, either."

"Then we better get up and call the island. I can't be the reason why my beautiful bride passes out from hypoglycemic shock."

Abby eased up her hips, and I regretfully slid free of her. On wobbly legs, she got out of the hammock. I followed quickly behind her. I wrapped my arm around her waist not just for support, but because I couldn't imagine going one second without touching her. Yeah, I was that crazy in love with her.

Chapter Eight

"Abby"

One Year Later

As the buzzing hum reverberated through my ears, I pinched my eyes shut and bit down on my lip. "Hang in there, Angel," Jake said, his voice cutting through the pain.

I squeezed hold of his hand. Being too much of a chicken, I didn't want to watch the needle entering my skin. Sure, I had drawn blood from countless people in nursing school, but this was different. This was...me. *My* skin. *My* blood. *My* pain.

"Damn, you're going to look so sexy with this ink," Jake mused.

My eyes popped open to stare into his twinkling blue ones. "You think?"

"Mmm, I'm pretty fucking sure."

"Please, with the way you act around her, she could wear a Hefty bag, and you'd want to bang her," Steve, Jake's favorite tattoo artist, teased.

"Can I help I married a woman who is sexy as hell?" Jake countered with a cocky grin.

Steve snorted. "Not touching that one, dude. You'll just wanna kick my ass if I say anything about Abby."

"Or tattoo 'Property of Jake' on her forehead," another artist quipped.

Jake rolled his eyes. "She *is* mine. Aren't you, Angel?"

I gritted my teeth through another round of needle pain before I responded. "You're so cute when you're a possessive caveman."

Jake nipped my bottom lip with his teeth before giving me a lingering kiss. I guess most people would have found our one year wedding anniversary gifts to each other a little odd, but I was thrilled beyond belief to finally be getting a tattoo. I'd talked about doing it since I'd first met Jake, but like a lot of things, the time hadn't been right. For some reason, I'd decided that my foot and ankle were the places I wanted to start with, which of course were the worst for pain.

"Okay, we're done outlining," Steve said.

Peeking open one of my eyes, I gazed down at my foot. "Oh wow," I murmured, as I took it all in. It was a vine of flowers that also included a butterfly. The vine itself was made up of lines of song lyrics as well as scripture I liked. It started across the top of my foot and went all the way up to wrap my ankle.

"Think you're going to live through the coloring?" Steve teased.

Oh God, there was more? I gulped. "I'll be fine."

"Maybe you should give her a leather strap to bite on," AJ suggested from his chair across the room. When I glared at him, he chuckled. He and Mia were also getting more ink as well. For AJ, it was having Mia and Bella's name written on his chest above his heart, and for Mia, it was an infinity symbol on her wrist with AJ's and Bella's initials.

"Don't listen to him, Abby. He about pissed his pants when I did his half sleeve," Becs, the only female tattoo artist, said with a grin.

"Whatever," AJ replied.

As Steve started in on the pastel coloring of flower, I gritted my teeth. Focusing on Jake, I eyed the temporary tattoo on his pec. "It sure was luck that your left side was the side you hadn't gone crazy with the tattoos," I remarked.

"I knew I was saving it for someone special," Jake replied, with a wink.

"Yeah, I bet."

As the needle tapped along my skin, I stared at the cursive lettering over Jake's heart. In a few hours, he would have *Angel* forever inked on him. It didn't bother me that it wasn't actually my name. Everyone knew who Angel was. There was no mistaking that it was anyone other than me. The very thought caused a surge a love to pulse through me.

When I looked back over the last year, I had so many wonderful memories to reflect on. It had sped by in a bliss-filled blur of mine and Jake's love. We remodeled the house to make it more into Jake's and my home, rather than Susan's. In between tour stops, we returned to our honeymoon island to have some alone time. Sure, we'd had our arguments and disagreements about everything from paint choices to my wardrobe. Now that we were married, Jake suddenly wanted my stage dresses to be longer and show less cleavage. Basically, he would have been happy if I had gone out on stage in a nun's habit. That was probably the longest we hadn't spoken to each other since our honeymoon blow-up. I'd even slept on AJ and Mia's bus because I was so pissed at his Neanderthal ideas. He'd come around the next morning with flowers and a grand apology. Mia had snatched Bella up and taken her for breakfast in the diner before our vigorous makeup sex could scar her.

While it had been a wonderful year, it had also been stressful, intense, busy, and at times absolutely manic. Another album released and another cross-country tour had meant more and more time away from home. Jake had finally consented to bring furry Angel along with us because I was so homesick for her. Having a dog on our bus was definitely interesting, but it inspired Mia to bring Jack Sparrow along on hers and AJ's bus. Miraculously, the two animals got along pretty well when we all hung out together. Both seemed united in their protectiveness of Bella.

Jake's and my duet, *Music of the Soul*, shot to number one the day it was released, and everyone was talking about a repeat win at the Grammys. The label was looking into booking our European tour. While I should have been the happiest woman on the face of the earth, something was missing. Deep down I knew what it was, but I didn't dare voice my longing to Jake or anyone else. I just tried to keep the faith that one day I would have the desires of my heart— one day I would have a baby of my own.

In the meantime, I channeled my maternal instincts into spoiling Jude, Melody, and Bella. I was also thrilled when Brayden and Lily announced that they were going to have a third, and final, child. Bray had finally talked Lily into buying their own bus and using her teaching degree to homeschool the kids while we were out on tour. The guys of Runaway Train were positively domestic now with their wives and children along. Only Rhys was still unattached. He spent his time on the bus with my brothers, and I didn't even want to know what kind of bachelor debauchery they were up to.

Just when I thought I couldn't take any more of the shading, Steve eased off. As he traded out colors, a sharp pain in my side caused me to grimace and suck in a breath.

"Hey now, I wasn't even doing anything," Steve said.

"I know. It's not you," I moaned.

Jake's brows furrowed. "What's wrong, Angel?"

"It's my side, down low. I keep having these pains."

"You should get them checked out."

"I'm sure it's just a cyst. I used to get them all the time when I was younger. Of course, I thought the birth control was supposed to stop them since I wasn't ovulating."

Now it was Jake's turn to grimace. "Um, seriously, babe. TMI."

I cocked my head at him. "Oh please. Like you can't hear the word ovulation."

"I'd prefer not to."

With a teasing tone, I said, "Ovary…fallopian tube…uterus."

"That's enough," he said, with a shudder.

"You're too funny getting all riled about the female reproductive system."

"Just promise me you'll get it checked out."

I held up my hand like I was swearing an oath. "As soon as we get back to Atlanta, I'll go see my doctor."

"Good." His fingers caressed my face. "I don't want to think of anything happening to you, least of all, you being in pain."

"You're so sweet and good to me," I murmured, as I gazed into his eyes.

A gagging sound came at my feet. When we glared at Steve, he held up his hands. "Sorry. But it's hard for me to do this when I think I'm going to puke."

"Douchebag," Jake muttered, which caused Steve to grin.

I held out my hand to Jake, and like the wonderful husband he was, he took it and squeezed encouragingly. "Best anniversary present ever," I said, with a smile.

"How will we top it next year? Sky diving?"

I shuddered. "Not with my fear of heights."

"Go back to our island and stay naked for days."

Steve cleared his throat. "What?" I asked.

"Are you trying to kill me? That statement either puts a totally inappropriate picture of Abby in my head—" At Jake's low growl, Steve shook his head. "Or, I see you and your naked ass parading around. Neither is a win-win situation."

"Finish the damn tattoo," Jake ordered.

Steve narrowed his eyes. "You forget that I'm working on you next. Don't make me take out my aggression on you."

Becs stepped up with an ink gun in her hand. "Why don't I help things along and take care of Jake?"

"Then I can't hold his hand for support," I whined.

Jake grinned. "Besides, this twatcanoe," he motioned at Steve, "is the only one who does my ink."

"He really doesn't think a woman can do it," AJ called.

"Shut up, dickweed," Jake muttered. He glanced at Becs and shook his head. "I appreciate your offer, and despite what that asshole over there says, I have confidence in your work, despite the fact you're a chick. But my lovely wife needs me, so I'm staying here."

I smiled. "My hero."

"No more talking, especially the lovey-dovey shit," Steve instructed.

"I thought the customer was always right," I countered.

"Not in my parlor," he replied, before he brought the needle back to my skin.

I sucked in a breath as Jake hovered over me. His breath warmed against my ear. "As long I whisper to you, Mr. Jackass can't get his panties in a twist," he whispered.

"Thank you," I replied.

"Do you know what I'm going to do when I get you home and into our bed?" After I shook my head, he replied, "I'm going to strip you down and bury my face between your legs until you scream my name."

His words caused my face to flush as well as a tingle between my legs. He continued to whisper all the naughty things he intended to do to me and for us to do when we got back home. By the time he finished, Steve was done with the shading of my tattoo. As I sat up to admire it, I secretly hoped there wouldn't be a puddle of wetness left on the chair that Jake's sexy words had induced.

"Like it?" Steve asked.

"I love it. It's amazing."

He gave me a genuine smile. "I'm glad you like it. It's always an honor taking one's tattoo virginity." While I laughed, Jake gave a contemptuous grunt. "Your turn," Steve said pleasantly to Jake. As Becs put on a thin layer of ointment and got ready to wrap my foot, Jake sat down in the chair opposite me to get inked.

As the needle entered Jake's skin, he met my gaze. His dark blue eyes burned with desire, and I felt my cheeks flushing. "Remember everything I said earlier?" My breath hitched as I bobbed my head furiously. "Just as soon as we get home. Every. Single. Thing."

A shiver of anticipation and need went over me. "What about your chest and my foot?" I dared to ask.

With a sexy grin, he replied, "Where there's a will, there's a way."

I had never wanted a tattoo to be finished more than I did his because I knew I had an amazing night waiting for me.

After a multi-orgasmic, all-night sexathon, Jake and I barely made it to the bus at seven am when the caravan was pulling out for the next tour stop. We immediately headed straight for the bedroom and crashed. The following day we pulled into Louisiana. Between my foot and ankle aching from the tattoo and my side continuing to hurt, I felt like ass through most of the morning's rehearsal. The instant we were through, I streaked off the stage, desperate for some Advil. I barely gave Jake a fleeting kiss before heading for the bus. Once I had stripped down to my sweatpants and a T-shirt and thrown back some pills, I headed over to AJ and Mia's bus for some downtime with Bella.

Coloring pictures and watching movies helped to take my mind off the pain. But when dinner rolled around, I was hurting so badly I couldn't eat. As I swept my full plate into the trash, Mia eyed me. "Are you okay?" I could tell her spidey-nurse senses were tingling.

"Just a little achy from the tat and then there's this stupid pain in my side."

"Which side?"

"Right."

"You still have your appendix?"

"Yeah. This is an intense, dull ache. Not like the typical stabbing, shooting pain of an appendix."

Mia crossed her arms over her chest. "Intense and dull sounds like an oxymoron, but I get what you're saying."

"I'll be okay."

"You sure about that?"

I sighed. "Look, if it gets too much, I'll go to the emergency room after the show, okay?"

"You better."

I couldn't help smiling at her expression. "You're so bossy."

"I'm a certified nurse. I don't have the option not to be bossy." Her lips quirked up in a smile. "Plus, I'm married to AJ. We both know he needs a firm hand."

I giggled. "Yep, you got that one right."

Jody, one of our bodyguards, poked his head in the bus. "Abby, it's time for you to go to the arena to get ready."

"Hope you feel better."

"Thanks," I replied, before heading down the stairs to follow Jody. The Advil I'd taken before I tried to eat dinner kicked in, and I felt a little better while Marion was doing my hair and makeup. But by the time the show started, the pain was back with a vengeance. As I sang and danced and interacted with the audience, I wanted nothing more than to just lie down.

The show went by in a blur, including when Jake came out for us to do our duets together. When we finished our last song, Jake took the microphone and smiled into the audience. "You guys ready to get rid of us yet?"

The roar of the fans grew even louder to the point where my ears rang with the noise. He turned to me and grinned before leaning back into the microphone. "Maybe the lovely Mrs. Slater and myself could be persuaded to sing just one more song."

Usually, the first act left the stage during set changes and house music played. Jake and I had talked about doing something to keep the fans engaged between the shows. It was also a way to bridge the musical gap between Jacob's Ladder, which was country rock, and then Runaway Train, which was pop/rock. Since Jake had learned guitar at his grandfather's knee to all the classic Johnny Cash songs, he suggested we do a little bit of Johnny and June. I had just enough sass in me to capture June's show style, so I was all for it.

After we finished our set of duets, we then sang *Jackson* together. I usually really got in to the performance, wagging my finger at Jake, playfully shoving him, giving him lip that went along with the lyrics, but tonight, as I handed off my guitar to a roadie, the pain in my side raged so hard I didn't know if I would be able to perform. During my set with Jacob's Ladder, it had grown even more intense. I'd even popped four more Advil during our costume change. The last thing I wanted to do was have to go the emergency room in some random city, but at the same time, I knew if it wasn't better by morning, then I had to go.

When the last chord echoed through the stadium, Jake leaned over and kissed me. "Give it up for my own little spitfire!" I forced a smile to myself as the audience roared and clapped.

"And to my very own Johnny sans all the black clothes," I said.

The roadies took Eli's guitar while Gabe came out from behind the drum set. "Show some big love for Jacob's Ladder!" Jake shouted into the mic.

Sandwiched by my brothers, I clasped both their hands before bowing. I had to grit my teeth when it came time to pick myself up. It took everything within me to smile into the microphone and say, "Goodnight everybody and God Bless!"

Jake gave me a brief kiss before heading off the opposite side of the stage for his entrance with Runaway Train. When I started off stage, the pain in my side grew so intense it caused me to stagger momentarily. Once I had regained my footing, I drew in a few deep breaths before continuing into the wings. Gritting my teeth, I wove in and out of the roadies and stage crew. As I bypassed the backstage waiting room, Eli called to me. "Where are you going?"

I glanced over my shoulder. "Back to the bus. I want to lie down."

Eli's brows furrowed. "You okay, sis? You look kinda pale."

Since I didn't want to worry them unnecessarily, I nodded. "I'm fine. I just need some more Advil that's all and to lie down for a little while."

"Jody, make sure Abby gets to the bus okay," Gabe instructed.

I rolled my eyes at their being so overprotective. "Guys, I'm fine."

"Just shut up and let Jody do his job," Eli replied.

Since the pain had grown even more intense, I merely nodded. In silence, Jody followed me to Jake's and my bus. Without the driver, Jody had to unlock the door. "Perry is inside with the rest of the crew. Will you be okay by yourself?"

"I'll be fine."

"Okay, I'll lock the door behind you."

"Thanks," I murmured.

When I started up the stairs, I felt something trickling between my legs. Pain seized me so hard I bent double and screamed in agony. My knees gave way, and I collapsed onto the floor. With trembling hands, I felt of the stickiness that ran down my thighs. Bringing it up to the light I saw it was dark red blood. "Oh God," I muttered.

Reaching out, I grasped hold of the side of the couch and tried to pull myself up. I knew my cell phone was somewhere in the bedroom, and I desperately needed to get to it. When I flung myself onto the couch, the stabbing pain caused me to shriek again. On trembling legs, I took two steps. A roar came through my head as everything grew black. I pitched forward and fell to the ground before everything faded around me, and I was enveloped in the darkness.

When I came off stage after our set, I was a sweaty, exhausted mess. Peering around the back stage room, I searched for Abby, but I couldn't find her anywhere. During our duets, something had been off with her, and I was worried. "She went on to the bus after our show. She wasn't feeling well," Gabe informed me.

Icy apprehension ricocheted through me. Abby wasn't one to ever complain, so the very fact she had gone to lie down meant there was something wrong. "Oh okay," I mumbled, raking a shaky hand through my hair.

When a roadie thrust a clean shirt and bottle of water at me, I shook my head. "Thanks man, but I'll grab something on the bus. I wanna check on Abby."

The roadie nodded as I brushed past him out the door. "Wait up, Jake," Perry, our bus driver said. I slowed my fast pace as he jogged up to catch me. "Figured I better come with ya since Jody locked her in."

I was glad Perry didn't give me any shit about starting out without a bodyguard. As I eyed the bus in the distance, I was surprised to see there weren't any lights on. A feeling of dread entered the pit of my stomach, and I couldn't help breaking into a run. When I reached the bus, Perry was right at my side. Once he unlocked the door, I pounded up the stairs. As I gazed wildly around the living area, my instincts had been spot-on because something didn't feel right. "Abby?" I called.

When she didn't answer, I started down the aisle. My shoe hit something firm in the middle of the aisle floor. I jerked my gaze down, and my world to shudder to a stop. Abby lay crumpled in a heap. I dropped to my knees at her side. "Abby?" After I pulled her into my arms, I patted her face several times, but she didn't open her eyes.

"Call 911!" I shouted at Perry.

He ripped his phone out his pocket and was dialing within an instant. My wild gaze took in Abby's unconscious form. At the sight of the blood on her thighs, my heart shuddered to a stop. "Oh, God. No." I rubbed Abby's arms and gently shook her shoulders. "Angel, please wake up. Please…don't leave me."

The piercing wail of the on-site ambulance filled my ears as did the glaring red and white lights. The next few seconds seemed to crawl by in a painful haze. As I cradled Abby in my arms, loud voices came from the front of the bus. The paramedics shoved me to the side as they started working on Abby. I barely felt Perry lifting me up and pulling me out of the bus. He dragged me down the stairs to where my bandmates stood.

"What's happened?" Brayden demanded.

"I dunno," I murmured absently, staring at the pavement.

Perry, whose arm around me was probably the only reason why I was still standing, spoke up. "She was unconscious on the floor when we got there. There was…blood."

A feminine gasp caused met to raise my head. Mia stood beside AJ with Bella on her hip. "You need to tell them that she's been experiencing lower abdominal pain, right flank, the last few days."

"Could it be her appendix?" Rhys questioned.

Mia shook her head. "Not if she's hemorrhaging. It sounds like something reproductive like a..." Her eyes widened, and she pinched her lips shut.

"Like a what?" I demanded.

"A miscarriage," she replied in a whisper.

I sagged against Perry. How could Abby be pregnant? She was on the pill, and most mornings, I saw her take it. "No method is one hundred percent," Mia said softly, as if she were reading my mind.

It was then the paramedics brought the stretcher down the bus steps, which was no easy feat. Even in the dim lights from the arena, Abby's face appeared ghostly pale. Without a thought, I raced to her side. "Is she..." My voice choked off. I couldn't even form the words I feared so much.

"No sir. She's stable. Her vitals are strong, but we need to get her to the hospital for some scans to see what's causing the bleeding."

"Can I ride along with you?"

"Sure," the paramedic replied.

His partner hurried to the cab of the ambulance and cranked up. I glanced back at the others. "Go on. We'll be right behind you," AJ said, and Brayden and Rhys nodded.

"Thanks," I murmured, before trailing behind Abby's stretcher. Once she was loaded inside, I hopped in and slid across the bench to sit beside her. I grabbed her hand, the one with her glittering diamond engagement ring and platinum wedding band, and squeezed it in mine. "I'm right here, Angel. I'm not going anywhere."

For the first time, I noticed she had a reaction, even though it was just her forehead crinkling. When he pressed on Abby's stomach, she shrieked and tried to turn away. "Stop it! You're hurting her," I cried, trying to push him away.

"Sir, I have to check your wife's injuries. If you don't stop, we'll have to restrain you, so you don't prevent us from doing our job."

With a defeated wail, I buried my face in my hands. If I could have, I would have plugged my fingers in my ears just like a child, so I didn't have to hear Abby's cries. When I glanced up again, she had quieted, and I saw the paramedic tossing a hypodermic into the medical waste bin. "Just something to help ease her pain."

"Thank you." I once again took Abby's hand in mine. I brought it to my lips and kissed it gently. The rest of the way to the hospital, I spoke softly to her in between fielding a barrage of questions from one of the paramedics. With the drugs in her system, she rested easily on the stretcher.

I didn't know where we were, least of all which hospital they were taking her to. I found out soon enough it was St. Augustine Memorial. When the ambulance doors flung open, a doctor and a nurse were already there, waiting on us. I don't know if it was standard protocol or if it was because Abby was famous.

After they took Abby from the ambulance, I trailed along beside her into the emergency room. When I started into her room, a tall nurse with auburn hair stopped me. "Sir, I'm going to have to ask you go out to the waiting room, so we can ascertain your wife's condition. We'll come and get you when we know more."

I shuddered as I felt a horrible sense of Déjà vu coming over me from the last time I'd been in this position. I remembered that horrible night when Bree, an ex-groupie of mine, in a jealous rage had almost killed Abby. She had been beaten so severely it had taken weeks for her to recover.

Now we were back almost in the same situation—a strange hospital, Abby being worked on by doctors and nurses, and me alone in the waiting room, wondering if the woman I loved more than anyone else on the earth was going to be taken from me.

AJ and Mia suddenly appeared, followed by Brayden and Rhys. AJ sat on one side of me while Mia sat on the other. I don't know how much time went by as I sat there staring into space, tuning out all the conversation around me. It seemed like an eternity before a middle-aged, male doctor in a white lab coat appeared.

"Are you Jake Slater?"

"Yes, I am."

"I'm Dr. Miller. I'm the physician assigned to your wife's case."

I swallowed hard. "How is Abby?"

"She's being prepped for emergency surgery."

"W-What?" I demanded, my heart shuddering to a stop before restarting.

"After an ultrasound and CT-scan, we discovered that Mrs. Slater had a large ovarian cyst rupture. This caused the hemorrhaging that she experienced."

"So you're going to operate on her to stop the bleeding?"

"Yes, but we will also need to remove her ovary and fallopian tube."

"Oh…fuck. But why?"

"It seems that during the growth of the cyst, it caused torsion or twisting with the ovary. That, along with the rupture, caused too much damage to the ovary and fallopian tube. We will also remove her appendix while we're in there as it has also suffered damage."

In the past, I had kept my knowledge of the female reproductive system to an as needs to know basis. That was one of the reasons I wasn't entirely clear what the doctor was trying to tell me. I did know that whatever they were taking out was part of what made babies. That thought alone caused a deep ache to burn through my chest.

"After this surgery, can Abby…can she still have a baby?" I croaked.

"Yes, the left ovary and left fallopian tube are not damaged. Usually, the remaining ovary will compensate for the lost one. It will depend on if there is any further damage from the hemorrhaging. Although she is young and healthy and could conceive on her own, I wouldn't rule out the use of IUI or IVF in the future to help matters along."

"I see," I murmured. Oh, fucking hell. My poor Angel…if only I had gotten to her quicker, maybe there would have been less damage.

"You and your family will want to go on up to the surgical floor waiting room. As soon as she is in recovery, a doctor will come out and tell you how the surgery went."

Once Dr. Miller left, the adrenaline in me depleted. My muscles felt rubbery, and they wouldn't support my weight. I collapsed back into my seat and buried my head in my hands. I shuddered at the smell of blood of my hands. *Abby's* blood.

Oh God, Abby was going into emergency surgery…she might not be able to have children like we planned. It was all too much, and I moaned in agony.

At the feel of Mia's hand on my back, I tensed. I didn't want her words of sympathy, nor did I want her comfort. I just wanted to be alone, so that I could somehow muster the strength to enable me to put on a brave face for Abby.

Mia soft voice came close to my ear. "Jake, I'm so, so sorry."

Twisting my shoulders, I slung her hand off me. "Just leave me alone."

"Hey man, I know you're hurting, but the last thing you need to do is to shut down. It isn't good for you and it isn't good for Abby," AJ said.

I jerked my head up to glare him. "Don't you dare try to tell me what's good for Abby. I'm her husband. I know better than anyone what she needs. As hard as it's going to be, I know I have to be strong for her right now because I know the minute she comes out of surgery and hears this news, she's going to fall apart. She's wanted a baby with me practically since the moment we met. And now I have to go in there and try to pretend that everything is all right when she may never get what she wanted."

Mia reached over and took my hand in hers. "I know the prognosis isn't the best in the world, but the doctor didn't say Abby couldn't have children."

"What do you two know about anything? You weren't even trying and bam, you got pregnant. Hell, neither of you even wanted kids. There's nothing Abby wants more than to have a baby, and now that's going to be a fucking struggle for her."

AJ narrowed his eyes at me. "Fuck you, man. Just because Bella wasn't planned, it doesn't mean we love her any less or that we didn't want her. Last time I checked, there isn't some pissing contest about who deserves what."

I snorted contemptuously. "Obviously because Abby sure as hell deserves a baby more than some whore who got knocked up!"

The moment the words left my lips I instantly regretted them and wished I could take them back. I grimaced when Mia gasped in horror while wounded tears welled in her dark eyes. Before I could say I was sorry, AJ's fist cracked into my jaw, sending me spiraling backwards. It had been a long time since I'd felt the power of AJ's right hook, but damn if he still didn't have it.

But he didn't stop with just a punch. He popped me in the abdomen, too. Stars flashed before my eyes as Brayden and Rhys scrambled to pull AJ away from me.

"AJ, stop!" Brayden cried.

As I rubbed my aching jaw and clutched my stomach, AJ shoved Brayden off him. His face was blood-red, and his eyes were wild with fury. "He called my wife a whore! He's lucky I don't break his fucking neck!"

"Leave him alone, Bray," I muttered as I pulled myself to my feet. I staggered away from the group, making my way to the elevators. I wasn't sure where in the hell I was going. I just knew I couldn't stay here anymore. Even I if I said I was sorry, it was going to take some time to get AJ to cool off. But, I sure as hell felt bad for what I had said to Mia.

I stumbled onto the elevator going down, which I felt made a hell of a lot of sense considering my mood. Digging in my pocket, I pulled out my phone and proceeded to make the call I was dreading.

I didn't know if in their shock, Gabe and Eli had managed to call their parents. Laura, Abby's mother, answered on the first ring. "Jake, is something wrong? We have some missed calls from Eli." I tried as best I could to explain what was going on.

As she burst into tears, I cringed. "We'll be on the next plane out. If we don't make it before she comes out of surgery, please tell her how much we love her, and we're trying to get there to be with her."

"I will."

After I hung up, I wandered around the lobby. At the sight of the chapel, I dipped inside. St. Augustine's wasn't big on religious diversity or having an interfaith chapel. Instead, votive candles flickered on a table underneath a lit cross.

I eased down on one of the back benches. I didn't know exactly what I was doing here. I hadn't come here for soul searching or to unburden myself. I just wanted to escape. Heaving a frustrated sigh, I turned and then lay down. I stared up at the ceiling, trying to sort through the emotional shit-storm that raged within me. I don't know how long I lay there, ignoring the beeps and pings of my phone. Minutes. Hours. An eternity seemed to go by.

My ears perked up at the sound of someone coming in the door. As they hurried past me to the altar, I craned my head back to look at them. It was Mia. When her back was to me, I rose up on the bench, eying her movements. She knelt before the altar and made the sign of the cross. Taking a candle, she bowed her head. "Heavenly Father and Holy Mother, please watch over Abby. Protect her through the surgery and carry her through the recovery. Most of all, bless her and her womb." A flicker a light came from the wick as the candle burning for Abby caught light. I expected her to turn around then, but instead, she took another candle. "And please comfort and protect Jake."

Her words had the same effect as AJ punching me, except this time I felt it in my chest, rather than my chin. "I don't deserve that," I croaked.

At the sound of my voice, Mia jumped and whirled around. Her face flushed. "I-I didn't know you were here."

"Yeah, I thought it was better if I laid low until after the surgery was over."

Mia chewed her bottom lip before coming over to sit down beside me. An uncomfortable silence hung around us for a few seconds. Finally, she broke it. "I'm sorry AJ hit you."

I shook my head. "Don't be. I'm sure as hell not. I deserved it. I said some really horrible shit to you two." I gazed into her widened, dark eyes. "I'm really, really sorry, Mia. That was a horrible thing to say to you. You know I don't, and have never thought of you as a whore. I have no idea why I said that. More than anything, you're an amazing wife and mother." I brushed my hand over my face. "God, I don't know what came over me."

Mia exhaled the breath I suppose she had been holding. "You were in pain. And like a wounded animal, you struck out at those who were just trying to help you."

Tears stung my eyes. "Abby would be fucking floored at what I said. All I do is disappoint her." I furiously shook my head. "I'm no good for her."

Reaching over, Mia took my hand in hers and squeezed. "That's not true, Jake. Abby loves you with all her heart and soul."

"Sometimes I think I'm a curse for her."

"What?"

"She was almost beaten to death because of me and now fucking this happens."

"Oh Jake, you're not a curse. You love Abby and would never do anything to hurt her. She knows that too." When I opened my mouth to protest, Mia brought her hands to my lips to silence me. "The last thing Abby would ever want is for you to be thinking like you are. Bad things happen to good people every single day. What happened with the cyst happens to thousands and thousands of women. You had absolutely nothing to do with it. Abby told me she'd had cysts before. She could have had it checked out when she first started having pains, but she didn't. Even so, she's not to blame either. Shit just happens."

With a defeated sigh, I let my head fall back. Once again, I found myself staring up at the ceiling. "You're right."

"Of course I am."

When I jerked my head to gaze at her, Mia smiled. I laughed and shook my head. "You really are the perfect match for AJ."

At my words, her smile grew even wider. "Thank you. I love him with all my heart."

"I can tell. I'm glad he found you."

"See, there's the sweet Jake I'm used to."

My brows shot up. "You really think I'm sweet?"

"Most of the time, yes. You can also be an arrogant, self-absorbed dick sometimes, but for the most part, you're pretty sweet."

I laughed at her honesty. "Yeah, you're right."

"Most of all, you're a caring and devoted husband. Anyone can see that. And one day, you'll be a wonderful father."

All the fears about becoming a father, letting my future children down, and cheating on Abby raged in my chest, and I drew a ragged breath. "I hope so."

Mia's phone dinged in her pocket. "Sorry, I need to check this. I left Bella with Frank."

I chuckled. "She'll be fine. He'll spoil her rotten by giving her too much sugar and not putting her to bed."

She smiled as she peeked at her phone. "It's AJ. He wondered where I was. They're upstairs in the surgical waiting room." She rose up and tucked her phone back in her jean's pocket. Then she held out her hand. "Come on. Let's go."

I grimaced. "I dunno if that is such a good idea."

"You don't need to be alone right now, Jake. We're your family." When I started to protest, she shook her head. "AJ loves you. He's had some time to cool down. Just tell him you're sorry, and I'm sure everything will be fine."

"I hope you're right."

She cocked her head at me and smiled. "Don't you know by now that we Runaway Train women are always right?"

I laughed. "Yeah, I think I do." I rose off the bench and then followed her out the door to the elevators. When we walked through the door of the surgical waiting room, AJ's eyes bulged at the sight of us. He glanced from me to Mia and threw her a questioning glance.

"Everything is fine," she assured him.

While he nodded his head, he still stood up and came over to wrap his arm around Mia's waist protectively. After raking my hand through my hair, I sighed. "Sorry, man. What I said was so fucking wrong. I've apologized to Mia, and she accepted it. I hope you can, too."

His dark brows furrowed while he surveyed my words. "Don't ever go there again. I don't care what's going on in your life—I'll end you, I swear."

"If I ever do such a douche thing again, you have my permission." I took a tentative step forward. "You're my best friend in the whole world. I never, ever want to hurt you or anyone you love. Okay?"

"Okay," he said. With a tentative smile, he gave me a hug.

"Mr. Slater?" a voice questioned.

AJ released me, so I could whirl around. I stared questioningly at the young male doctor in the doorway. "Yeah?" I croaked, my heart shuddering to a stop.

He smiled. "Your wife came through the surgery just fine. We were able to stop the hemorrhaging, and the removal of the tube and ovary went well. She's in recovery, and you can come and see her in a few minutes."

I closed my eyes and staggered back until AJ caught me. "Thank God," I murmured. Once I could breathe regularly again, I pulled away from AJ. I stared around the group of my band mates and Abby's brothers. "Thank you all for being here. For loving me and Abby so much." I couldn't fight the tears anymore, and I broke down. AJ's arms came around me as well as Brayden and Rhys's. They didn't tell me to man-up or call me out for being a pansy. Instead, they just patted my back, spoke soothingly to me, in an acceptable man-way, and let me cry. We truly were brothers in that moment.

After I'd pulled myself together, a nurse came to take me to Abby. I followed her back through the maze of rooms to where Abby was. Her eyes were closed, and her face was as pale as the white sheet she had drawn to her chest. I eased down in the chair beside her and took her hand. "Angel?"

Her eyelids fluttered as she tried to wake up. "I'm right here, babe." I squeezed her hand reassuringly.

She stared up at the ceiling for a moment before her head slowly turned to look at me. A smile formed on her lips. "Hey."

The sweet sound of her voice sent warmth through my chest. I leaned in to kiss her hand. "Hey, yourself."

Her gaze swept around the room, taking in the machines, and she shuddered. "Am I okay?"

"Yeah, you are now."

My words didn't console her. Her lip trembled as tears pooled in her eyes. "Can I still…"

I was sure she didn't know much of what had happened, but it wasn't hard to believe her first thoughts would be to worry about having a child. "Yes, you can. And we will someday, I promise."

"Sooner than later?" she whispered.

In my heart of hearts, regardless of what had just happened tonight, I still wasn't ready. But I knew I would be a real bastard to say that while Abby lay recovering from major surgery. So, I forced a reassuring smile to my lips. "Of course, Angel. As soon as the doctor says you're ready."

The lie left a bitter taste in my mouth, but I wouldn't have taken anything for the beaming smile that lit up Abby's face. I dreaded the day that I had to disappoint her again.

Chapter Ten
"Abby"

Nine Months Later

Sometimes you spend so much time pretending that you forget what real is. That's exactly what happened to me in the weeks following my surgery. The strong hold I had on being positive began to slip. The "what-ifs" began to plague me, and anxiety sent me reeling. But while there was a storm brewing within me, I appeared calm and serene on the outside. No one would have ever guessed how much torment I was in. I had a smile permanently carved on my face although I was becoming hollow on the inside.

Everyone wanted the positive, happy, and sweet Abby, and that's exactly what they got. I threw myself into touring and promoting our new album. When I was home, I worked constantly on making our house into a home for not only Jake and me, but for our family and friends. If I stopped for just an instant, the voices of doubt grew more intense. So I stayed as busy as I could.

But I knew there would be a breaking point—a reckoning day when it would all come crashing down on me. And when it finally came, I never imagined how heart-wrenching it would actually be…

"What do you think about this one?" I asked, as I held up a beautiful bouquet of delicate pink roses.

"Looks good," Jake mumbled, barely taking his eyes off the magazine he was reading.

I grinned and rolled my eyes. Jake could have cared less what flowers we got for Lily and Brayden. He was completely out of his element in the hospital gift shop. He had zoned out the moment we stepped into the baby section, and while I was busy smelling flowers, he had ducked away to grab the latest issue of Entertainment Weekly.

"Okay then, we'll get these for Lily and Brayden, and now we need something for the baby."

Jake's brows furrowed as he brought his gaze from the magazine to mine. "I thought we already gave them a present."

I waved my hand dismissively. "That was at the baby shower. We can't go in empty handed."

With a sigh, Jake glanced at the shelf full of stuffed bears, rabbits, and other woodland creatures. He grabbed up a plush, white teddy bear with a giant pink bow on it. "There. Now we have something."

"You can carry that, and I'll take the flowers."

"I'm not carrying this bear."

"And why not?" I questioned on my way to the register.

"Because I'll look like a pansy," he hissed.

"You'll look perfectly normal on the maternity floor."

He grumbled behind me, but after the cashier rang up the bear, he took it back and tucked it under his arm. "Thank you," I said.

He grinned. "You're welcome."

We headed out the door to get on the elevator. Brayden and Lily's daughter had been born around midnight last night. While it was a wonderfully exciting occasion, it was also hard because we were set to leave this afternoon for the Southern leg of tour, which started in Alabama. Brayden would have to leave Lily and his newborn daughter behind for an entire week. Luckily, both his parents, along with Lily's mom, were coming into town to help out.

We got off on the fifth floor, which was maternity, and quickly found Lily's room. "Knock, knock," I said, as I pushed the door open.

"Hi guys," Lily said. Reclining on the bed with a mountain of pillows, she held a newborn to her chest. Jake's steps momentarily faltered in the doorway when he thought Lily might be breastfeeding, and I couldn't help but laugh.

"Coast is clear."

He rolled his eyes. "Whatever," he mumbled, although I could see the relief in his eyes.

As we stepped closer to the bed, I couldn't believe how good Lily looked after just giving birth twelve hours before. Her smile was radiant as she glanced at her beautiful baby, swathed in a pink crocheted blanket I was sure Mia had made. "Brayden will be back any second. He took Jude and Melody to get an ice cream in the cafeteria."

"And who do we have here?" I asked.

"This is Miss Lucy."

"Well, that's Lucy Sky to be exact," Brayden said from behind us. He grinned as he and the kids came inside.

"Jesus, dude, another Beatles reference?" Jake asked.

Lily laughed. "He got lucky this time because my grandmother was Lucy."

As I stared down at Lucy in Lily's arms, I couldn't fight the overwhelming urge to hold her. Deep down, I knew it wouldn't be good for me, but I couldn't help myself. "Can I?" I asked Lily.

"Of course," Lily replied, as she passed Lucy over to me.

The sweet scent of newborn innocence filled my nose as I held Lucy. She continued snoozing as I took in her diminutive features. "She's absolutely gorgeous," I murmured.

"She looks just like me when I was a baby," Melody said.

Jake peered over my shoulder at Lucy. "Yeah, she does."

Brayden grinned. "She's got Mel's dark hair, that's for sure."

The door burst open to announce the arrival of AJ and Mia. While AJ held Bella in his arms, Mia had an armful of balloons and flowers. "We couldn't wait to see the newest member of the Runaway Train family," AJ said with a grin.

"Thank you, man," Brayden said, before giving AJ a hug.

Rhys poked his head in the room. "Is this where the party is?"

Brayden laughed. "Sure is. Come on in."

Rhys sidled up to me to get a look at Lucy. "Wow, you've got another stunner on your hands. Better look out for her in sixteen years."

"Yeah, I think she and Melody will be giving me a lot of grey hairs," Brayden replied.

AJ nodded. "I hear ya, man. If this baby is a girl, I think I'm going to have to invest in some early hair care prevention."

"This baby?" Lily and I asked at the same time.

Mia huffed out a frustrated breath before smacking AJ's arm. "You weren't supposed to mention the baby today! It's about Brayden and Lily, not us."

AJ's expression turned sheepish. "Sorry. My bad."

Bella clapped her hands. "I gonna be a big sister!"

Mia glanced around at us. "Fine. Since Mr. Blabbermouth and my daughter can't keep quiet, yes, I'm three months pregnant."

A hearty "Congratulations!" went up around the room.

Next to me, Rhys groaned. "Oh God, *another* baby? What happened to us being a band of rockers? Now we're a band of dirty diapers and Dora. I mean, seriously guys, we're going to have to have a separate eighteen wheeler to get around all the crap for your kids."

"Shut up, jackass," AJ replied.

As the happy conversation buzzed around me, I didn't hear any of it. I was too overwhelmed by the news of Mia's pregnancy coupled with holding new life in my arms. Mia and Lily had what I desperately wanted, and the green-eyed monster of jealousy was rearing its head.

Sensing my jangled emotions, Lucy's face scrunched up, and she began to cry. "Guess I better give her back now," I said, before handing her to Lily.

"Shh, sweetheart. It's okay," Lily cooed softly, and within a few seconds, Lucy was quiet.

The walls of the room seemed to close in around me, and I fought to breath. I knew I had to get away, or I was going to lose it and start screaming. I bolted for the door when Jake reached out to grab my arm. "Where are you going?"

"Just to the bathroom," I lied. I forced a smile to my lips before I slipped out of the door. Fighting the tears, I started putting distance between myself and Lily's room. Somehow I ended up down the hall at the nursery. There were only a few babies inside since most were in the rooms with their mothers. Leaning in, I placed my hand on the glass.

A newborn baby boy slept peacefully wrapped in a tight cocoon of blankets. The name on his bassinet read, *West*. He had a head full of dark hair, and even in his sleep, his mouth worked on a phantom pacifier.

"Abby?" Jake questioned softly from behind me.

I didn't turn and look at him. Instead, I kept staring at the sleeping baby. "Did you know that I wanted to be a Labor and Delivery nurse?"

"No, I didn't."

With a nod, I replied, "If I had finished my degree, that's what I had planned on doing. I couldn't imagine anything more fulfilling than helping to bring life into the world."

Jake took a tentative step towards me. "Look, I know you're upset about seeing Lucy and then the news of Mia's pregnancy."

A mirthless laugh escaped my lips. "Makes me a horrible person to be jealous, doesn't it?"

"No, I think it's only natural for you to feel that way. Kinda like when I see guys and their mothers. We can't help what we want."

"No, we can't."

"Maybe…maybe we can start trying for a baby."

Although Jake's words should have been music to my ears and the answer to a prayer, they instead just brought pain from something I'd been carefully hiding. "It won't work," I whispered.

"What do you mean it won't? We haven't even tried," he protested.

My eyes snapped shut in pain. With the walls of my carefully constructed façade starting to crumble, I figured I had no reason to continue harboring my horrible secret. "I have to tell you something, Jake."

"What is it?"

"I've been lying to you," I choked out.

His dark brows furrowed in confusion. "About what?"

I slowly turned to face him as my heartbeat began to race out-of-control. "I stopped taking my birth control a few months ago right after I was cleared from my surgery."

Jake stared at me in disbelief. "What?"

"I wanted a baby, and I knew it was going to be harder to conceive. You said after I came out of surgery, that when the doctor cleared me, we would try. So I thought…I thought if it took us a long time to get pregnant, then you really would be ready then. Then at the same time, the waiting and the wondering if I could was too much to bear."

The color drained slowly out of Jake's face. "You *promised.* You swore to me on our honeymoon that you would never do anything so horrible as to go behind my back."

Tears pooled in my eyes before streaking down my cheeks. "I know. But things changed with my surgery—"

"Not enough to make you lie to me."

"I'm sorry, Jake. I'm so, so sorry."

He shook his head. "I can't believe it."

"You don't understand what the last nine months have been like for me. I wanted to believe everything would be all right, but I couldn't. And then I couldn't talk to you about it because I knew how you really felt about having a baby."

"So you're trying to make this my fault?" he shouted, which caused a few nurses to turn their heads in our direction.

"No, I just want you to try to understand why I did what I did. I want you to see that even though I wasn't thinking straight, there was a reason."

"A reason for you to deceive me?"

"Please, Jake," I begged.

He stared at me before shaking his head again. "It's like I don't even know who you are anymore."

When AJ appeared before us in the hallway, Jake pointed a finger at him. "Take Abby home. I can't be around her right now."

Sobs overcame me as I watched Jake stalk down the hallway to the elevators. AJ's comforting arms came around me. "Shh, it's going to be all right."

Something deep within me wondered how it ever could be. After all these months of deception, I had somehow known that Jake would react the way he had. Even though I knew his anger and his hurt would cause him to walk away, I hadn't changed my mind or come clean. And now, I had to live with the consequences.

The scenery became an emerald blur, as I stared out the window of the bus. It was kinda ironic, as the last few hours, after I'd stormed away from Abby at the hospital, had been a painful blur as well. Well, painful didn't quite cut it. In the moment, it had been fucking agony hearing her admit to stopping her birth control, and now hours later, the ache still hurt so bad it was hard to breathe.

I hadn't gone home or even to our apartment in the city. Instead, I had just walked around downtown Atlanta—gone to Centennial Park, watched the kids playing in the water fountain. A few people recognized me and asked for autographs, but for the most part, I was isolated and alone in my torment. I'd finally headed back when it was almost time for the bus to pull out.

Abby had stood beside our bus with Angel on her leash. Her eyes were puffy and swollen from crying. "Jake, please, talk to me," she began, but I kept walking right past her. Instead, I did what I did best, which was basically shut people out and be an asshole. I had climbed onto AJ and Mia's bus without a word to her.

At the sight of me, Mia raised her eyebrows to AJ, but neither one of them said anything. I eased down at the table where Bella was eating a snack and coloring. "Want some?" she asked, pushing the plate of animal crackers my way.

"No thanks, sweetheart."

Out of the corner of my eye, I saw AJ and Mia having a quiet, but heated discussion. She threw her hands up before stalking over to me. "I think you're lost."

"Excuse me?"

She narrowed her dark eyes at me. "I said, I think you're lost. This isn't your usual bus. You remember, the one you and your *wife* ride on."

I glanced over at AJ who shook his head like he wasn't about to get into it with Mia by taking my side. "Please Mia, I need some time, okay?"

She huffed out a frustrated breath that ended almost in a growl. "What I would say to you right now if it wasn't for her," she said, pointing to Bella. She then stalked away from me over to the kitchen, and for the next hour, she ignored me. But I didn't really mind as long as she wasn't yelling at me. I focused my energy on staring out the window and trying to process what in the hell had happened to my life.

When I felt a tug on the pants leg of my jeans, I glanced down to see Bella staring up at me. She had abandoned her place on the couch with AJ where they had been watching movies. "Hey sweetheart," I said. I bent over to pick her up and ease her down on my lap. Her jet-black eyes surmised me before she cocked her head at me.

"Why u sad?" she asked.

Great, I didn't even begin to imagine how I was going to explain this one. "Do you think I'm sad?"

Her dark ponytail bobbed up and down as she nodded. Leaning over, her tiny hands came to my cheeks. Her fingers gripped my flesh before she pushed my face up. "Smile, Unca Jake."

I laughed through my smushed cheeks. "Okay, okay. I'll smile instead."

A pleased little grin spread on her face. Grabbing a piece of paper off the table, she waved it at me. "I dwawed u a picture."

"You did?"

"Uh, huh."

As I stared down at the scratchy, multicolored drawing, I knew better than to make any assumptions about what was on there. I'd made that mistake when Jude was little and caused him to burst out crying when I suggested the drawing of me was a dog. "So tell me about the picture," I urged.

Her little finger stretched out to one of the stick figure/semi blobs. "Dat's u and Dat's Aunt Abby."

"I see. Oh, you did a really good job." She had managed to give the Abby blob yellow hair and mine brown. My eyes honed in on the yellow and brown blob beside us. "Is that…Angel?"

She giggled. "No."

"Oh, is it your kitty, Jack Sparrow?" At the mention of his name, the one-eyed Siamese cat lifted his head from his perch over the table and eyed me contemptuously.

"It's u baby," she said, as if it was the most obvious choice in the whole-wide world.

I sucked in a harsh breath. After today, Bella's comment was like a double roundhouse kick straight to the groin. "But I don't have a baby, sweetheart."

"But u will. Evewy night before I go to sleep when I say my pwayers, Mommy and I pway for you and Aunt Abby's baby."

I cut my eyes from the drawing to stare at Mia. An unapologetic smile appeared on her face before she quickly looked at Bella. "Come on, pumpkin. It's time for your nap."

"No," Bella protested, burrowing down in my lap. Her fingers twisted into the material of my T-shirt as if I was her lifeline to keep her out of naptime hell.

AJ crossed his arms over his chest, looking seriously parental. "You know the rules, mi amor. If you don't take a nap, you don't get to see me at the show tonight."

Bella squirmed in my lap. She, along with Jude and Melody, loved nothing more than to put on their noise-blocking headphones and stay backstage, watching us perform until their bedtime. Leaning over, I whispered into her ear. "Go on and take your nap. I'll need to see you at the show so you can make me smile," I urged.

"Okay," she said. Before she hopped down, she gave me a smacking kiss on the cheek. "'Mon, Jack," she instructed. Although the cat hated me and AJ with a passion, he had a special love and patience for Bella. He rose up and stretched before hopping down. Once Jack Sparrow was at her side, she put her tiny hand in Mia's and started down the hallway to the bedroom. Glancing at me over her shoulder, she said, "Love u, Unca Jake."

"Love you too, princess."

Once the door was shut behind them, I exhaled the breath I'd been holding. As AJ eased into a seat across from me at the table, I gave him a shaky smile. "Your daughter is far too smart for her own good."

He laughed. "Tell me about it. It's like she's two and a half going on twenty-two."

An uncomfortable silence then passed between us. I could hear Mia reading Bella a story. Finally, I cleared my throat. "So Abby was pretty upset when I left, huh?"

AJ grimaced. "I'd say emotionally obliterated."

My chest ached at the prospect, and I sighed raggedly. "She fucking blindsided me, man. To find out she's been lying to me these past few months. That she ended up doing what I feared the most—what she swore she would never do." Gritting my teeth, I shook my head. "How can I ever trust her again?"

"Look man, I know that it all seems pretty desperate right now. But you have to sit back and think for a minute. Abby has stood beside you through some pretty heinous shit—times when you were hard to love and did things that she didn't understand or maybe approve of. But she stayed right by your side, man."

"I never openly deceived her like this," I protested.

"Would you just take a second to think about it from her perspective? She goes through a pretty horrible surgery, she's worried to death about having a baby, something you know she wants more than anything in the world, so what does she do? She cracks and does something that goes completely against her character."

I stared down at Bella's drawing, taking in AJ's words. "I'm not saying what she did wasn't wrong, Jake. It's a hard pill to swallow when anyone lies to you. But at the same time, you have to look at the bigger picture. She wasn't cheating on you or stealing money from you. She wanted a baby—something she said you gave her hope for after her surgery."

"I wasn't thinking straight that night. I didn't want to hurt her after her surgery, so I lied."

AJ's brows rose up. "Oh, so it's okay for you to lie, but it's not for her?"

"Fuck," I muttered, rubbing my hand over my face.

"You have to talk to Abby. I know she's sorry for what she did. She loves you so much that she would never, ever do something to hurt you."

"But she did."

"You lied to save your own skin. She lied because she was so incredibly scared. When she did, it wasn't out of spite, but desperation."

I raised my brows. "Is there a fucking difference?"

AJ snorted. "I sure as hell think so. It was out of desperation that Mia handcuffed me to that shower. She doesn't have a spiteful bone in her body." He gave me a pointed look. "And neither does Abby."

"But—"

Holding up his hand, AJ killed any argument I had with his next words. "Wasn't it desperation that drove you to say the hateful things you said to try to drive Abby away when Susan was dying?"

"Yeah," I croaked.

"Then I rest my case."

"Would you forgive Mia if she had done the same thing?"

AJ didn't even hesitate before replying. "Under the circumstances, yes, I would." He then narrowed his eyes. "And then I would fucking man-up and stop denying the love of my life what she wanted most in the world."

I gave a defeated sigh. Maybe AJ was right. Maybe I needed to be the man and husband Abby needed and give her what she wanted. Wasn't marriage supposed to be about compromise and sacrifice? Abby had been doing a hell of lot of that, but I hadn't gotten with the program yet. "How do you do it?"

His brows furrowed in confusion. "Do what?"

"The father thing. How do you do it now, and how did you not totally lose your shit when Mia got pregnant?"

AJ shrugged. "I don't know. I mean, sure, I freaked out when I found out Mia was pregnant. I couldn't sleep for worrying how much having a baby was going to change my life. Did I really want my life to be changed? Did I really want the responsibility of some little person? But in the end, the answer was yes, I did. Maybe deep down, I always knew I wanted kids. Then at the same time, I had to put my fears on the backburner because I was fighting for Mia. I wanted a life with her and my child so much that I guess it took away some of the fear. Yeah, there were days where I'd wake up in a sweat, scared to death that I was going to fail Mia and Bella. And once Bella was born, I began worrying about her constantly. But that's what being a father is about."

"How do you know if you're ever ready to be a father, though?"

AJ laughed. "Most guys never do, and even if you think you're ready, you're really not." He cocked his head at me. "Why are you so scared of being a father?"

"Too many fucking reasons," I muttered.

"Yeah, well, hit me with some of them."

I threw up my hands. "Fine, but don't say I didn't warn you."

"I'm listening."

"I seem to hurt the ones I love, so I'm afraid of something bad happening to my kid."

"That's not true, Jake. Bad things happen every day. You can't help who they happen to. Susan dying of cancer wasn't your fault. Abby getting beaten and then having the cyst, not your fault either. Your kid may have asthma or break his arm falling off of a bike, but that isn't your fault either."

I wrung my hands in my lap, afraid to voice to AJ my ultimate fear. Under his intense stare, I finally caved. "I'm afraid I'll become my father. I'm afraid Abby will be so consumed by the baby that she won't care about me the same way, and when I don't have her undivided love and attention, I'll look for it elsewhere."

AJ shook his head. "Damn."

"Yeah, pretty fucked up, huh?"

"How did you ever get something like that in your head?"

I glanced down at the table and prepared to tell AJ something I hadn't even told Abby. "One night after my parents divorced, my dad was drunk. Really drunk. It was one of the first nights I'd ever stayed with him at his new apartment. He and Nancy weren't married yet. When I went to get something to eat, he cornered me in the kitchen." I closed my eyes as the memory that had haunted me for years overcame me. "He said, 'I know you hate me because of what I'm doing to your mom. But everything was fine between Susan and me until you came along. She always loved you more and put you first. I always came second, so I went to find someone who would put me first'."

When I dared to look up at AJ, his eyes were wide with shock. "That's fucking…ball-busting."

"Yeah, I know."

"But damn, man, he was drunk when he said those things."

"Isn't there a little truth behind every drunken statement we make in anger?" I countered.

"Maybe." AJ scratched the stubble on his chin. "But for the most part, Mark isn't a major douche. I doubt he seriously felt that way. The man was drunk, and his whole life was imploding around him."

"Whatever," I muttered, wishing for a bottle of Jack right about now.

"Have you ever talked to your dad about it?"

"No. Never."

"I think you should."

I snorted. "You think if I have some magical Dr. Phil chat with my dad, that all my fears about being a father will just go away?"

"No, but I think it's a good place to start." He rose out of his chair. "I'm going to go back and lie down with Mia and Bella. That'll give you the privacy you need."

"AJ, I don't think this is the kind of conversation you do over the phone."

"I agree, but I think you've waited too long to do it in person. Might as well do it now."

I watched his retreating form go down the hall and into the bedroom. I warily eyed my phone on the table. With a ragged sigh, I picked it up and scrolled through my contacts. When I got to my dad's, my thumb hovered over the send button as I debated my decision. Finally, I manned up and pressed the button.

My dad answered on the third ring. "Hey, it's Jake."

"Hey son, how are you doing? Abby still doing okay after her surgery?"

"Uh, yeah, I'm fine…she's fine." I swallowed the knot of emotions forming in my throat. "Actually, Dad, we're not okay."

"Did you have a fight?"

"It's a little more serious than a fight."

"Whatever it is, I know it's worth working out. Abby's a wonderful, caring woman, and she loves you very much."

"I know."

"Then, what is the problem?"

"I need…I need to talk to you about some pretty heavy shit that happened in the past. With you and me." There was a pause on the line. "Are you still there?"

"I'm here." Dad sighed. "I've been hoping you would want to talk to me for a long, long time."

"I doubt you'll be thinking that in a minute."

"I'm serious, Jake."

"Fine. Here it is. I've hurt Abby because I'm not ready to be a father, and it's all because of you."

Dad sucked in a harsh breath that hissed over the line. "No beating around the bush, huh?"

"I'm sorry, but I don't know how to talk about this—I never have. But having kids and being a father is about to ruin my marriage."

"I wish I could be there with you right now, son."

Before I could stop myself, I blurted, "Wanna hop a plane or drive and meet me in Birmingham?"

"If you want me there, I will."

My brows shot up into my hairline. "You're serious?"

"Of course I am."

"But why would you do that for me?"

"Because you're my son. There isn't anything I wouldn't do for you."

It took a moment for his words to set in. I knew from the tone of his voice that he was serious. It was just hard to imagine after all the years that have passed and all the shit between us, he really did love me. It was a lot to process with everything else that had happened today, and I felt myself shutting down. "It's okay. We can talk when I get back."

"I know I made a lot of mistakes when I divorced your mother—I said and did things that I know hurt you. I wish I could take them back, but I can't. The worst thing in the world would be to know that I hurt you so deep you wouldn't become a father. At the end of the day, you aren't me and you aren't Susan. You're just yourself, your own person."

"So I won't feel tied down and cheat like you did?" I questioned softly.

Dad was silent for a moment. "Is that what is bothering you?"

"Maybe."

"Oh Jake, what's going on in that head of yours?"

"A lot of bullshit, I guess."

With a nervous chuckle, Dad said, "I would like to think it's just bullshit, but I know you too well. All I can say is we're our own people and make our own decisions—good and bad. If I were to speculate long term about you, I don't see you cheating."

"And how can you guess that?"

"Because you know what a good thing you have. Before Abby, you were with enough women to know what is real and what is good. Deep down, you know you don't need to go anywhere else to find the greatest love of your life—the woman who completes you, challenges you, and makes you get up in the morning."

Like a pansy, tears stung my eyes at his summation. He was right—I could never find another woman who meant as much to me as Abby did. After all, she is my world.

The biggest question that was going through my head was on the tip of my tongue, and I knew I needed to ask it. Even if the answer was one I didn't really want to hear. Finally, I drew in a deep breath and croaked, "Do you think I'll be a good father?"

"I know you'll try as best you can. When you fall short, and trust me, you will, you'll beat yourself up. No one is a perfect father—some are better than others and some make less mistakes, but no one is perfect. You live and you learn."

"I hope you're right."

"All you can do is try your best, son. Regardless of how you see yourself, you have so much love to give to a child. I know that, and Abby knows that as well."

The shuddering of the bus's wheels slowing down alerted me that we were getting off the interstate and heading into downtown Birmingham. "Listen Dad, I gotta go for now. I really appreciate you talking to me."

"I'm here for you anytime, Jake."

"Thanks." I hesitated at the next words, hating myself for how hard they were to say. "I...I love you."

"I love you, too."

After I hung up, I sat in silence just staring at my phone. I didn't know if I should try to text or call Abby. Part of me knew that what I had to say needed to be said in person. Because of Lucy's birth, we were heading straight into a show, rather than having our usual rehearsal times. I wasn't going to have a moment before going out on stage to talk to Abby unless I cornered her in the dressing room.

Any thoughts I had of getting to her on the bus was shot to hell when I saw her brothers walking her into the arena. I sighed and went to get a shower. When I was finished, Bella was bouncing around the kitchen waiting for me to come out.

"Guess you had a good nap, huh?"

She grinned. "I did."

AJ rolled his eyes. "She never sleeps long enough."

Mia yawned. "No, she doesn't."

"I'll see you later, okay?"

AJ and Mia gave me a questioning look, and I nodded. They both smiled. "Go get her," AJ said.

I laughed and then headed down the aisle. After pounding down the bus steps, I headed into the arena. As I started in the dressing room, Marion was talking with Frank. He must've asked her how Abby was because she was shaking her sadly. "Poor thing. She was an absolute mess. I never thought I would get her ready and out on that stage. Her eyes were so bloodshot and swollen I wasn't sure I could make them look okay. I must've used two tubes of concealer."

At the sight of me in the doorway, Marion clamped her lips shut and whirled around. "Ready for me?" I asked, when I caught her gaze in the lighted mirror.

"Sure," she replied curtly.

It goes without saying that she was firmly Team Abby. She raked her nails a little harder into my scalp than she usually did, and the times when she usually patted on the stage makeup, she smacked my face instead. "I'm going to make it right," I said softly.

She glared at me for a moment. "You damn well better."

"Or you'll take my balls?"

She grinned wickedly. "Yeah, something like that."

I laughed. "Then I better do it fast, huh?"

"Exactly."

When Marion finished with me, I didn't lounge around in the backstage room. Instead, I made my way to the stage. I needed to see

Abby. It'd been a long time since I'd actually just watched her perform. Just the sight of her in her sparkly, ice-blue stage dress and silver cowboy boots made my heart race. To the average eye, no one could tell there was something off with her performance tonight. She shimmied and shook her hips as she danced along with the music while her smile remained bright. She had the audience laughing in between songs at her little jokes and stories. But when she turned away from the audience, the pain on her face was visible. The consummate performer within her wouldn't allow for her to give anything less than one hundred percent.

"We're going to do a cover right now of an artist who means a lot to me and my brothers. Growing up, our mom was a huge Emmy Lou Harris fan. Even in the remote jungles where we were living, she had old records she would play. *If I Needed You* was one of the first secular songs I learned to play on the guitar. So Eli and I would like to sing it for you now."

Eli eased down on the stool beside her with his guitar, and then they began harmonizing together. As I took in the lyrics of the song, I realized how much they were Abby's and my relationship. But the one that meant the most was "If you needed me, I would come to you. I would swim the seas for to ease your pain."

Abby had always been there for me in my darkest times. Then when she was going through her own, I hadn't realized her suffering. She'd had to go it alone, and that was so wrong. I'd vowed at our wedding to love her in the good times and bad. Regardless of what she had done with going off birth control, she had needed me, and I hadn't been there. I had to make it up to her. I knew what AJ and my dad said was true.

After the song ended, applause and cheering rang throughout the auditorium. I knew this was my usual cue to get to the wings to await her announcing our duets. She took the microphone. I noticed her boot tapping on the stage floor, and I knew she was nervous about seeing me.

"And now, I want to bring someone to the stage to sing with me. I think you all know him pretty well. And that would be my husband, Jake Slater."

While the crowd went wild, I stepped out on stage, my guitar slung over my shoulder. I waved to the audience as the roadies fixed the stools for Abby and me to sit on during our first song. Once they scurried away, I sat down. "Hello Birmingham! How the hell are you?"

Deafening applause and whistles erupted around me. "You been treating my lovely wife and her brothers well?" Once again they clapped and screamed. "First up tonight, we want to sing one of the first songs we ever did as a couple. It's called *All I Ever Needed*."

I strummed the opening chords, and Abby came in with me. Instead of looking at me, she kept her eyes down. When we got to the musical break, I stared intently at Abby, willing her to look me in the eye. But she kept staring down at her guitar. Pushing the microphone out the way, I took her chin in my fingers and titled her face up. When her gaze met mine, I smiled. "I'm so sorry, Angel."

Her eyes widened. "Y-You are?"

When we didn't pick up with the second verse, Eli and Gabe kept playing through the song. I'm sure they wondered what in the hell we were thinking for having a conversation in the middle of a performance. But I had no other choice. It was kind of weird have a musical interlude during your big apology scene.

I nodded. "Can you ever forgive me for the things I said? For lying to you?"

"Can you forgive me? For deceiving you?"

"I'll forgive you, and you can forgive me."

The corners of her lips quirked up in a smile at my words, but her expression remained grave. "Just like that?"

"I had a long time to think on the bus. And I talked to my dad."

"You did?"

"Yeah, I did. Things are…good now."

Tears pooled in Abby's baby blues. "Oh, Jake."

When I glanced out at the crowd, I saw their puzzled expressions. "What do you say we finish this song, and then we'll talk about it after the show?"

She grinned. "Okay, I think that sounds good."

I took the microphone back and stared into the audience. "Sorry about that, guys. My wife and I just needed a moment. Hope you didn't mind?"

At their roaring approval, Abby and I both laughed. I counted us in, and then we started the song where we had left off. I don't think I'd ever enjoyed performing with her more. Well, maybe the night at the Grammys before we won best duet. But tonight was special too. Nothing meant more than reconnecting. Nothing meant more than knowing she still loved me, despite my all my bullshit hang-ups and issues.

I stared intently at her when I got to the line, "Tell me it's not my fault."

Smiling, Abby shook her head and sang, "Tell me it's not my fault."

With a wink, I continued singing melody with Abby harmonizing. When the song finished, I popped out of my stool. After laying my guitar down, I pulled Abby into my arms. She abandoned her guitar to wrap her arms around me. Grabbing her under her ass, I hoisted Abby up to wrap her legs around my waist. The audience went wild, but I could have cared less. This moment wasn't about giving them a show. It was about repairing my marriage and making things right with the woman I loved. Even though I should have moved us off stage, I couldn't wait one moment to make things right with her. "I love you, Angel."

"I love you, too."

I stared intently into her eyes. "And I want you to have my baby."

She gasped. "You do?"

"Yeah, I do. I want us to make lots of babies together. I want them to have your sweet smile, your caring spirit, and your sassiness. I want them to be as beautiful on the outside as they are on the inside, just like their mother."

Abby's emotions overcame her, and she started sobbing. "Don't cry, Angel."

"You're so sweet, Jake. But what if…" Her eyes closed in pain. "What if I can't get pregnant?"

I shook my head. "You don't know that yet. The doctor said we might have to try other means to make it happen."

"You're willing to do that?"

"I'll do anything for you."

She brought her lips to mine for a frantic kiss. "Thank you, Jake. You've made me so happy."

"You make me happy every day, Angel." I kissed her again before pulling away. "What do you say we finish this show, so I can take you back to the bus and show you just how much I love you?"

She laughed. "I'd like nothing more."

With my Atlanta Braves cap pulled low over my eyes, I hunkered down in my chair in the waiting room of ARMC or the Atlanta Reproductive Medicine Center. It was thirty minutes after closing, and the place was pretty much a ghost town, except for a few patients straggling out from their appointments. Each time someone came out to the front desk, I tensed, fearful they would recognize me. Abby, who sat beside me, would squeeze my hand reassuringly. As I cut my eyes over to her, I couldn't help snickering at her disguise.

Her beautiful blonde hair was hidden underneath a jet-black wig. Her usually long hair was only chin length. Tortoiseshell glasses were perched on her nose, and her usually sparkling blue eyes were hidden under dark contacts. Of course, the disguise had been my idea. She hadn't given two shits about whether or not we were spotted a fertility clinic. "A lot of our fans suffer from this too, Jake," she had reasoned. But the prideful side of me didn't want to see our faces splashed all over the tabloids—our private agony on a grocery newsstand as people checked out with their milk and bread.

The ARMC's Perimeter location had become a familiar fixture in our lives since I'd finally decided not to be a selfish prick and consent to having a baby. Usually you had to go a whole year of not getting pregnant before you were referred to a fertility clinic. But because of Abby's surgery, we were a special case, and we got to cut the line.

She had been through a whole gamut of below-the-waist tests that I didn't begin to understand. I was sure that more people had seen her vag in the last two months than in the entire time she'd been on this earth. As modest as she usually was, she didn't seem to care her hoo-hah was on display for various specialists. For me, it helped that our doctor was a female, as were the technicians.

"Mr. and Mrs. Moore?" the nurse called.

It took Abby smacking my arm for me to move. For a minute, I didn't recognize the name. And then I remembered I was even more of a bastard because I had us under an assumed name—my mother's maiden name.

I scrambled out of the seat to follow Abby and the nurse down the hall. Once we were closed into the room, the nurse took my blood pressure and temperature. All the while, she and Abby chattered to each other while I remained silent. When a plastic cup was thrust into my hands, I totally froze. Even though there were words and sentences coming out of the nurse's mouth, I couldn't hear anything. I didn't nod in acknowledgment or reply. My gaze bounced back and forth between her and Abby. While Abby nodded along, I remained rooted to the floor, unblinking and unmoving.

When the door closed behind the nurse, my throat constricted. The walls of the room seemed to close in on me. I stared dumbly down at the container in my hand before glancing down at my junk. If my dick could have talked, it would have probably said, *Not on your fucking life am I about to get it up in this room for you to jack off into a cup! Have you lost your pride, dude?*

"Jake?" Abby questioned. When I glanced up at her, she wore a concerned expression. "Baby, are you okay?"

"Fine," I croaked.

"You look a little green."

That's probably because I feel like I'm going to puke. "I'm fine," I reassured her.

"You know I can tell when you're lying, right?"

I gulped. "Seriously?"

She nodded as she closed the gap between us. "It's okay to be freaked out about this, Jake. When it all comes down to it, I'm freaked out too."

"You are?"

"How could I not be? We're in a reproductive clinic under assumed names with me in a disguise."

"Yeah, that's true."

She swept the wig off, her blonde hair tumbling over her shoulders. After she tossed it on the examining table, she looked back at me and smiled. "But in the end, it's just you and me, babe. It's still the two of us making a life, even if the conception is a little different than what we planned."

"I know," I murmured, staring at the plastic cup in my hands.

"Jake, look at me," Abby commanded.

When I glanced up at her, she smiled. "I wanted to do something to make this easier on you." Her hands came to her top.

With wide-eyes and my mouth gaping open, I watched as she pulled it off. "Abby?" I croaked. I couldn't believe she was stripping down.

"We're in this together, Jake. Did you really think I was just going to make you do this on your own?"

"Well, um, maybe?"

She tsked at me. As I gazed at her checked bra, I realized it was familiar. Licking my lips, I could barely wait for her to strip down. As she shimmied the skirt off her hips and down her thighs, I couldn't help smiling.

She grinned back at me. "Recognize this lingerie?"

"Oh, yeah."

"I chose it for a reason."

"Besides the fact that I love you in it?"

"Mmm, hmm." She tossed her skirt onto the table with her sweater. "You know, we did something like this once before, remember? Me in this lingerie with you touching yourself."

"Um, it was a little different since we were both on the phone and weren't in the same room together."

"It's still kinda the same thing."

"If you say so," I murmured, as I eyed her garters. "Fuck, Angel, you're so damn sexy."

She gave me a wicked grin as her fingers came to the button of my jeans. After she unbuttoned and unzipped me, she slid my pants and boxers down to my knees. Although I was enjoying the sights, my dick still wasn't with the program. I couldn't help feeling a little embarrassed when Abby glanced down and saw. "It's okay," she whispered, her breath warmed against my cheek. "I'll take care of that."

I moaned when her hands came to grip my dick. As her hands worked up and down me, my cock slowly started to rise to the glorious occasion. I exhaled the breath I'd been holding. "Touch me, Jake," Abby murmured. With her free hand, she brought my palm to her breast. As I squeezed her flesh over her bra, she continued working my growing length.

With my free hand, I reached out to pull her closer to me. I wanted my lips on hers, but most of all, I wanted my tongue in her mouth. It was the closest I was going to come to being inside her today. As I thrust my tongue against hers, Abby moaned into my mouth. I slid my hand into the cup of her bra to knead one luscious breast. My thumb tweaked her nipple into a hardened point as Abby sped her pace up on my dick. As I continued plunging my tongue in and out of her mouth, I felt my balls tightening.

"Come for me, Jake," Abby commanded, her breath hot against my mouth.

Since she'd never said those words to me before or with that demanding tone, I could do nothing else but obey her. Burying my head in her shoulder, I shuddered and convulsed. When I finally came back to myself, I glanced down. In a hoarse voice, I questioned, "Did I make it?"

"Yep, we have a cup full of baby batter!"

I laughed. "Is that what we're calling it?"

She grinned. "It's better than a cup of cum, isn't it?"

"Yeah, I think so. Although I'm digging the alliteration of it."

Abby kissed me. "Thank you, Jake."

"You're welcome, Angel."

She smiled as she pulled away. She then capped the container and hurried to get dressed. I pulled up my boxers and jeans before heading to the bathroom. After Abby and I washed up, the nurse appeared to take the container.

"So what happens now?" I asked.

"After the semen analysis, it will then be frozen in preparation for the IUI procedure." She glanced over at Abby. "Which should be in a few days, right?"

"Yes," Abby replied.

The nurse nodded. "Then we will unfreeze the sperm, wash it, and then prepare for the IUI. Then hopefully, you'll be pregnant."

"I hope so," Abby murmured.

"The next step is to call us when you get your LH surge, and we'll go from there." With one last smile, she headed out the door with our baby batter.

"How about dinner?" I asked, as Abby grabbed her purse.

"After all of that, how can you think about food?"

I snorted. "I just worked up an appetite, babe."

She rolled her eyes. "You're impossible."

"Frankly, after you just used me like that, I think the least you could do was buy me dinner."

Abby grinned. "I think I can do that."

The morning of our IUI, I went in with Abby to hold her hand. I felt like I needed to be there not only to support her, but because it felt like I still had a part in conceiving our child if I was there. I couldn't believe how quick the actual procedure was. Sure, there was a lot that went into the "before" parts of the insemination, like Abby having to pee on an ovulation stick, take some egg producing drugs, get ultrasounds during her period and God knows what else. Then of course, there was my part of jacking off to get our baby batter, which turned out I had good swimmers. I mean, I wasn't too surprised at that fact.

But that morning, it was just a catheter shooting my jizz into Abby's uterus. She didn't even have to lie down for a long time afterwards. When it was over, Dr. McElroy gave us her kind, knowing smile. "Now, don't be surprised if it doesn't work out the first time. The window for conception really is smaller than anyone believes. Just because it doesn't happen this time, doesn't mean it won't."

I guess I should have taken more stock into that little pep talk. Especially when the early pregnancy test the clinic did revealed we weren't pregnant. Abby held out hope that maybe the test was wrong until she got her period. I found her a weeping mess in the bathroom, glaring at a box of tampons on the counter like they were the enemy.

Wrapping my arms around her, I let her cry it out. When her sobs had become nothing more than sniffling, I pulled away and kissed her. Cupping her face in my hands, I stared intently into her eyes. "Angel, it's going to happen. Remember what the doctor said."

"I'll try," she whispered.

I would like to say that the second time was a charm, but it wasn't. And each time we didn't get pregnant, more of Abby's hope died a little, and I saw the vulnerable, emotionally battle-worn side of Abby that few others did. She had been so good to care for me during my dark times, so now it was my turn. Each time, I spoke words of encouragement that the next time would work.

And then the fourth time it actually did.

Abby was really pregnant, and I was going to be a father.

"She's absolutely beautiful," I murmured, as I gazed down at the newest member of the Runaway Train family.

"That's because she looks just like her mother," AJ mused, kissing Mia's cheek.

"I can see some of you in there, too," I argued. "Just like with Bella."

Gabriella Maria Resendiz, aka Gaby, had been born at eight this morning, and she was just a few hours old. Unlike her older sister's limo birth, she had made a very casual appearance into the world by being born in a hospital on her actual due date. But you could hardly say there was anything ordinary about Gaby considering her father was a famous musician, and her arrival had beckoned a rag-tag group of paparazzi who had taken mine and Jake's pictures when we entered the hospital.

Mia glanced up from gazing lovingly at Gaby to smile at me. "So today's the day, huh?"

I returned her smile as my stomach filled with butterflies. Actually, they felt more intense like flapping seagulls beating against my abdomen. Today was our first ultrasound—the first picture of the little life Jake and I had fought so hard to get. I couldn't help being a nervous wreck. Since I was only seven-and-half weeks, I wasn't safe from the danger of miscarriage. That fact scared me to death. A terrifying fear there would be no heartbeat. "Yeah, we probably need to leave to make it to our appointment."

"It's going to be fine," Mia reassured me.

I nodded. "I hope so."

"It will," AJ insisted, thumping Jake on the back. "A few months down the road, your kid will be playing with Gaby on the bus while having Bella, Lucy, Melody, and Jude to entertain him or her."

The thought brought a smile to my face, and for just a moment, it helped me tune out the voices of doubt in my head. "That sounds wonderful. Thank you."

AJ winked at me before turning his attention back to Gaby's sleeping form. Jake's hand came to rest in the small of my back. "Ready, Angel?"

"Sure."

"You can't go without holding Gaby," Mia said.

I grinned. "Like you'd have to twist my arm."

She smiled as she passed the baby over to me. I leaned down to bestow a kiss on Gaby's tiny forehead. In Spanish, I whispered, "Bienvenido al mundo, hermosa, niña bendecido."

"Thank you for welcoming my beautiful, blessed girl," Mia said.

My brows rose in surprise. "Your Spanish is getting really good."

"After three years of AJ's random lessons on the bus, coupled with trips to Guadalajara, I've picked up a lot," Mia replied, with a grin.

With a final kiss, I passed Gaby over to Jake. He smiled as he nestled her against his chest. "I think I'd like for us to have a girl," he said, as he gazed at Gaby, whose eyes had popped open.

"Really?" I asked, to which Jake nodded. So far he hadn't said one way or the other what he wanted—just that he hoped the baby would be healthy. He was good with little girls—Melody, Lucy, and Bella all worshipped him. I tried imagining for a moment what our daughter might look like. "You think that now, but I wonder if you would be saying the same thing when she became a teenager," I mused.

Jake grimaced. "Yeah, that will blow." He glanced over at AJ and shook his head. "I feel for you, man."

AJ laughed. "It's going to be tough when they want to date, and I insist on going along with them."

Mia snorted. "Yeah, right. Like that will ever happen."

"We'll see," AJ replied, with a wink.

Jake kissed Gaby's head before passing her back to Mia. Then we made our goodbyes, and Jake took my hand and led me out of the room. We didn't have far to go since Mia and I went to the same OB, and the practice was around the corner from the hospital. After we signed in, we took a seat, and I nervously began tapping my foot.

"Abby Slater?" the nurse questioned. If I had been getting questionable looks from the women and men in the waiting room before, they were now on heightened alert that I was someone famous. I guess the fact Jake was sitting next to me didn't help. We hurried away from their prying glances and followed the nurse to the ultrasound room.

"Exciting day, huh?"

"Yes, it is."

"If you'll just go into the bathroom and slip off your jeans and underwear. Today's ultrasound will be transvaginal."

"Okay."

I took the flimsy sheet from the nurse and headed into the bathroom. Once I'd taken off my jeans and panties and deposited them on the hamper, I wrapped the sheet around me and headed back outside. On shaky legs, I got up on the examining table. After I was settled, my hand flailed out, searching for Jake's. When he grabbed it in his and squeezed, I exhaled a shaky breath.

The door opened, and the ultrasound technician breezed in. She glanced at my chart before she spoke to me. "Hi Abby, I'm Claire."

"Nice to meet you," I said, extending my free hand.

If Claire recognized who we were, she didn't let on, and I was glad. In that moment, it was kind of nice being treated normally. "So, let's get a picture of your baby," Claire said, as she sat on her stool and rolled up to the examining table.

Within a few seconds, the probe was inside me, and I gritted my teeth at the pressure. But all of that was forgotten the moment an image appeared on the screen. "Looks good," Claire murmured.

I had to agree with her as I stared at the pea sized image. "Wow," Jake murmured at my side.

"Oh, my," Claire said, peering at the screen.

"W-What do you mean?" I asked.

"Is something wrong?" Jake demanded.

Claire glanced from the screen to us and then smiled. "There's nothing wrong, so don't panic."

"Then, what is it?"

"I'm seeing two sacs."

My brows furrowed as I tried processing her words. "Two sacs…does that mean…"

"Twins," Claire replied.

The world spun in a dizzying flurry, and I brought my free hand to my head to try to still the spinning. "You did take fertility drugs, correct?" Claire asked.

"Yes, some Clomid to help egg production since I only have one ovary," I replied.

"Multiples with fertility medicine are quite common."

I glanced over my shoulder to stare at Jake. His face had paled considerably after our momentary scare. I couldn't begin to imagine what was going on in his head now. "Twins?" he croaked.

"That's what it looks like. Let's see if we can pick up two heartbeats." Claire began scurrying around to hook me up to a fetal heart monitor. I held my breath, hoping and praying that there would be two. I didn't know if I would have the chance to have another baby, so the idea of being blessed with two at once was overwhelming.

At the sound of our babies' heartbeats echoing around the room, tears stung my eyes. With one thump-thump, came another thump-thump. "There we go," Claire said.

"Oh, my God," I murmured.

Jake squeezed my hand. "You okay, Angel?"

Tears streaked down my face. "I'm more than fine. I'm absolutely perfect."

He smiled and kissed me. "You think we're up for twins?" he asked, in a shaky voice.

"Oh, I am, but what about you?"

Jake stared thoughtfully at the screen, eying our baby blobs. "I think it's the most amazing and most terrifying prospect in the entire world."

I laughed. "I couldn't agree more. We're truly blessed."

Jake smiled. "Yeah, we are."

In that moment, the happiness of carrying two babies outweighed any fear I might've harbored about being the mother of twins. After all, I would have a wonderful support system with the members of Runaway Train, along with my parents. Deep down, I knew that I could handle two babies at once, and that Jake could as well. He would rise to the challenge like he always did.

Chapter Fourteen
"Abby"

Two Months Later

After the initial surprise and shock of finding out we were having twins, life went back to normal. Well, I guess I should say normal for us. We'd had a blissfully wonderful month off where we'd spent time in the studio working on new songs, lounging around the house, and entertaining family and friends. Then, it was back out on the road touring the Midwest. We had just pulled into Salt Lake City the night before.

Jake had let me sleep in longer than I should have, and I was running late to rehearsals. I hustled off the bus and followed Jody into the arena.

When I got there, I found roadies bustling around, preparing for the show, but I didn't see my brothers. Searching out a familiar face, I found Frank. "Isn't it rehearsal time?"

"It's being delayed," Frank replied.

"What for?"

"So Loren can make some set changes."

"Set changes?" I asked dumbly.

Frank scratched the back of his head and refused to look at me. "Frank Patterson, would you please tell me what the hell is going on?" I demanded.

Frank sighed. "Fine. Jake asked Loren to make some set changes that would enable you to sit down and stay off your feet more during your performance."

"He didn't say a thing to me about this."

"Now, Angel, before you go getting all riled, Jake's heart is in the right place. He's a concerned father-to-be."

"He's an overprotective jerkwad," I mumbled, before stalking off. I must've looked pretty pissed because all the road crew gave me a wide berth as I made my way back to the dressing rooms. When I threw open the door for Runway Train's, AJ glanced up from his phone, took one look at me, and then let out a low whistle.

"That's our cue, man," he said to Rhys.

"Hell yeah," Rhys murmured, before they both scurried away, leaving me and Jake alone.

"What's wrong?" he asked, as he twirled a guitar pick between his fingers.

I threw up my hands in exasperation. "Oh, I don't know. Maybe the fact I just showed up to a rehearsal that isn't happening because Loren is busy doing set changes. Apparently I need to be on my ass more when I'm performing!"

Jake shook his head. "If you're expecting me to apologize for looking out for you and the twins, you're not going to get it."

"But Dr. Ghandi hasn't mentioned anything about me staying off my feet."

"That doesn't mean we can't take some precautions."

"Jake—"

He held up his hand. "You're not going to win this one, Angel."

I let out of frustrated growl as Jake rose out of his chair. "You can be such a stubborn ass sometimes, you know that?"

He grinned. "Hmm, I think I could say the same thing about you."

"I appreciate you being so protective, Jake, but I just wish you would have told me first. I hate being the last one to know."

Jake's thumb brushed along my cheekbone. "You're right. I should have told you first. At the same time, I had hoped Loren would be done by rehearsal time, and you could just go with the flow."

"And just what do Gabe and Eli think about your grand plan?"

When Jake winced, I knew he had already talked to them about it. "Once again, you should talk to *me* first. I'm your wife, and the one this all affects."

"I'm sorry, Angel. Will you ever forgive me?" He poked his lip out and gave me a puppy dog expression.

"Give me a kiss, and I'll think about it," I said, with a smile.

"You drive a hard bargain," Jake replied, before bringing his mouth to mine. Just the feel of his hard body pressed against me, his masculine smell, his strong hands on my waist, sent me into a frenzy. I gripped his shoulders tight, moaning into his mouth.

He pulled away and glanced at me with surprise. "Pregnancy hormones?" he questioned.

I nodded my head furiously up and down. "Would you oblige me in a quickie?"

"I'd love to." Prying himself off me, he went over to the door and locked it. He flopped down in one of the plush chairs and crooked his finger at me. With a grin, I walked over to him. He leaned forward and jerked down my panties, before pulling me down onto his lap to straddle him. Once I unzipped his jeans and sprung his erection, I raised my hips to bury him deep inside me. Wrapping my arms around his neck, I alternated between riding him hard and then slow.

I was getting close to coming when a knock came at the door. "Abby? Loren is ready for you now," Frank called.

"Just a second," I shouted back.

"Oh please, since when does it take me a second?" Jake replied with a wicked grin.

I tightened my muscles around him, causing him to groan. "We're cutting it short because I'm not letting Frank hear us."

Jake gripped my expanding hips and pushed me on and off him. I came almost instantly, and he followed shortly behind. Once I could focus again, I scrambled off his lap as best I could with my expanding belly and grabbed a towel to clean up.

When I opened the door, Frank took one look at me before his face turned blood red. "Uh, I...I mean, Loren is ready for you now."

"Thank you," I said. Glancing over my shoulder, I blew Jake a kiss before heading out the door to follow Frank to the stage. He gave me a pleased smirk.

As it turned out, Loren had done a pretty cool job integrating lit stools for Eli and me to sit on, and he'd also managed a pretty cool swing that went along with one of our backdrops. I was sure that Jake probably wouldn't be digging the swing since in his mind it could have mechanical failure, and I could fall. But I liked it, and I planned on using it. Of course, sitting in it and balancing a guitar with an expanding belly wasn't an easy feat. I was at four-and-a-half months now, and I couldn't imagine what it was going to be like when I was eight or nine months along.

At the same time, I knew there was no way in hell that even if my doctor let me, Jake would agree to allow me to perform late in my pregnancy. I figured I would have to cross that bridge when I came to it. For now, I was enjoying still being able to perform, and I didn't want that to end anytime soon.

"Don't you feel a little bit like we're cheating on Dr. G?" Jake asked, as we sat in a posh OB/GYN's office in downtown Salt Lake City.

I laughed. "She's the one who found this practice for me."

Since we were still in the middle of our Midwest tour, it had become necessary to find OB's along the way. For today, it was about the fact I didn't want to wait two more weeks to get home and find out what we were having. The suspense was killing me. I didn't know whether I should start buying two of everything blue or pink or blue and pink. So, my OB had recommended a practice for us to go for the gender sonogram.

When the nurse called us back, I could barely control my excitement. Unlike our first ultrasound, I wasn't scared or apprehensive. Instead, I was just so excited to find out what we were having.

The ultrasound tech, whose nametag read Jess, came in with her head buried in our chart. The moment she glanced up and took us in, she said, "Holy shit!"

"Guess she recognizes us," I murmured to Jake.

She grinned. "I thought the names on the chart sounded familiar but…wow!"

"Nice to meet you, too," Jake said, extending his hand.

With a trembling hand, she shook it. After staring at us for a moment, she finally pulled herself together and became professional again. "Right. Sorry about that. Totally lost my mind for a moment." Taking the bottle of gel in her hand, she squirted some on my exposed belly. "Let's see what we have here."

The grainy image of the twins came on the screen. I never tired of seeing them—their tiny hands and legs flailing, the sight of their hearts beating strong in their chests.

"So Baby A is a…" She glanced over at us, appearing to enjoy torturing us with the suspense. "A boy."

I squeezed Jake's hand and stared up at him. "We're going to have a son."

His response was to kiss me. When he pulled away, he smiled. "And the other baby?" he asked Jess.

"Looks like you're getting one of each—Baby B is a girl."

"Really?" I asked.

She nodded. "Everything looks really good with them—strong heartbeats, healthy placenta. Of course, it looks like your son is stealing a bit of the calories since he's bigger." She pointed to the screen to show us the difference.

"But she'll be all right, won't she?" Jake asked, his brow furrowed in worry.

"Yes, she'll be fine." Jess then printed a few pictures complete with baby A and B identified with their genders. When she finished, she gave me a towel to wipe off my belly. "Good luck."

"Thank you," I said, as I pulled myself into a sitting position.

When she got to the door, her hand hesitated on the doorknob before she turned back to us. "Would you mind signing something for me?"

"We'd be happy to," I replied.

We ended up signing a few pieces of paper before we escaped out the door. When we got into the limo, I took out the pictures to look at the twins again.

As he rubbed my stomach, Jake smiled at me. "Now that we know what we're having, what about names?"

"Hmm, good question. I know I want our daughter to have your mother's name."

Jake's expression pained as he stilled his hand on my abdomen. "That's really sweet, Angel, but I don't think I can bear calling her Susan. It would hurt too much."

I cupped his cheek with my hand. "Then we'll call her something else. What was your mother's full name?"

"Julia Susannah. Papa and Grandmother shortened it to Susan."

"That's a beautiful name for our daughter." I patted his hand on my belly. "What if we called her Jules? That's kind of a sassy little nickname. And if she's anything like your mom or me, she'll be sassy."

Jake grinned. "I agree. And I love that. Jules Slater sounds like a future rock goddess, too."

"It does."

"And for our son?"

"He needs his father's name in there somewhere."

Jake wrinkled his nose. "He's getting my last name. What about something of yours?"

I shrugged. "We could give him my dad's name as a middle name."

"Andrew's a good, strong name." He winked. "And biblical."

"So is Jacob," I countered.

Jake laughed. "Fine. We'll think about using my name as a middle name too."

"I like using family names and giving our babies history."

"So do I, but at the same time, I don't think you want to use my Papa's name."

I wrinkled my nose. "I love him, but I don't want to name our son Herbert."

"Neither do I."

Jake's phone dinged in his pocket, and he pulled it out. He read the text and grimaced. "What's wrong?" I asked.

"That was Loren. He's been researching the auditorium in Boise, and he thinks we're going to need to scrap doing *Jackson* or add in another song with it because the way the stage is built."

I gasped. "That's it."

Jake's brows furrowed. "What's it?"

"Jackson."

"You want to name our son after the duet we're doing?"

"Not entirely. My mom's maiden name is Jackson."

Jake appeared to be thinking about the name. "Jackson Slater…*Jax* Slater." He grinned. "I like that a lot."

"Jacob Jackson Slater," I said, with a smile.

He rolled his eyes. "Andrew Jackson Slater," he countered.

"Then it sounds like we named him after the president."

Jake laughed. "I guess you're right." He rubbed my belly. "So, Jax and Jules it is."

"I love it."

"And I love you."

After going through all I did to conceive, I never thought I would ever hate being pregnant. And then I crossed the eighth month mark, and true loathing of swollen feet, heartburn, sleepless nights, and waddling around began to grate on my nerves.

It probably didn't help that I'd been on bed rest for a month. The moment I stepped off the tour bus, my OB had banished me to the four walls of the master bedroom at home. Sure, I was tired and worn out from performing, but at the same time, it was hard laying around all the time when you were used to being on the go. Jake was good to spend time amusing me. We watched movies and ate our meals together. He also made sure I had female company by having my mom, Allison, and Lily come for visits.

Mia was good to come up for the day with Bella and baby Gaby. While I snuggled with the girls and watched movies, Mia worked hard knitting hats and booties for the twins. She and Lily also organized my baby shower, which turned into an epic event that included Jake, the guys from Runaway Train, the roadies and their wives.

Even though I hated being bedridden, I would have taken anything for it instead of having contractions six and a half weeks before my due date. Jake immediately called my doctor, and then we made the fifteen minute drive to the hospital. After doing an ultrasound, as well as an exam, my OB, Dr. Ghandi, had me being prepped for an emergency C-Section. The twins were in distress as my blood pressure had started rising. When the phrase "preempting any future preeclampsia" floated around, I went into panic mode, but Dr. Ghandi assured me that by getting the twins out, we weren't going to face that.

In a blur, I was wheeled from an examining room into the OR. Jake momentarily left my side to get outfitted in his scrubs, hat, and mask. When he returned, they'd already given me an epidural, along with some other drugs, and erected a sheet, so I couldn't see what was about to happen below my waist.

It felt like I was floating outside of my body. Tugging pressure came from below the sheet. I fought as hard as I could to say awake, but I felt myself drifting away into unconsciousness. "There he is!" Dr. Ghandi exclaimed. My droopy eyelids snapped open. Craning my neck, I gazed to where she held a wailing Jackson.

"God, he's so beautiful," I murmured, the oxygen tube moving tighter against my nose.

Dr. Ghandi passed Jackson to a nurse and then went back to work. My eyes cut across to where the nurses worked to clean Jax up. He appeared strong and healthy, and I wanted nothing more than to hold him in my arms and ease his crying. As if he could sense my thoughts, he turned his face toward me in the bassinet. "Hi sweetheart. Mommy's here," I called hoarsely.

"And here's number two!" My eyes cut from Jax over to Jules. I knew immediately something was wrong. While Jax had cried heartily, Jules was silent, her lips blue. A flurry of activity began happening below my waist.

"What's wrong? Why isn't she crying?" I demanded.

Once she was cut from me, Jules was handed over to the charge nurse. She began suctioning Jules's mouth while another nurse rubbed her tiny arms and legs. Tears blurred my eyes. "Jake!" I cried desperately. My arms were tied down so I couldn't touch him.

His tender lips came to kiss my cheek. "Shh, it's going to be okay, Abby. They're working with her. I know she's going to be just fine." But the fear burning in his eyes was palpable. The small amount of skin showing outside his mask was pale.

I closed my eyes. "Please Susan," I murmured.

"What sweetheart?" Jake asked.

I didn't reply. Instead, I just kept praying to Susan to intercede on Jules's behalf. I was still drifting between consciousness when Susan's face appeared before me, and she smiled. My eyelids snapped open at as the sweetest sounding cry in the whole wide world echoed through the room. "See, she's fine!" Jake exclaimed.

I barely got to see Jules's wailing form before she was ushered out of the delivery room. "Where are they taking her?" I asked.

"To the NICU. They can better regulate her oxygen levels there," a nurse replied.

I hated I couldn't have just a moment with her to see her up close, maybe kiss her cheek or hands. But I was also so thankful she was all right, and they were working to make her healthy.

As Dr. Ghandi worked below my waist stitching me up, a nurse appeared at my side with Jackson in her arms. "Would you like to meet your son?"

"Oh, yes. Please."

She laid Jackson gently on my chest where we were face to face. Jax strained to look at me. "Hi sweet boy," I murmured. His image before me became wavy as my emotions overcame me, and I began to cry. I wanted more than anything to be able to hold him—to unwrap his blanket and count his tiny toes and fingers.

Jake's thumb rubbed across Jackson's cheek. "He's pretty amazing, huh?"

"Yes, he is. I can't believe we made him."

With a grin, Jake said, "Once upon a time, he was just a part of some baby batter in a cup."

I laughed. "You're terrible."

"But you love me anyway, right?"

"Oh yes. I think I love you more today than I ever had."

Jake's warm lips met mine. "I love you so much, Angel." He bestowed kisses on both of Jax's tiny cheeks. "And I love you, sweet, little man."

"Why don't you go out and tell everyone the good news?"

"I'd rather stay here with you two."

"I'll be fine. They'll be taking him away to move me to recovery, where I'll probably snooze until the drugs wear off."

"Are you sure you don't want me to stay?" Jake asked.

I shook my head. "I know my parents are scared to death worrying about me and the twins. Go put them out of their misery."

"Okay." Jake bent over to kiss me once again. "You are the most amazing woman I know in the whole wide world."

I couldn't help laughing at his statement. "I'm not the first woman to give birth, Jake," I countered.

He shook his head. "You're the only woman I love who has."

"You say the sweetest things," I murmured.

"Only for you." He kissed me again and then started for the door.

I had only a few more moments of bonding with Jax before they took him away. As they wheeled me into recovery, my eyelids began to flutter, and it wasn't long before I fell into a contented sleep.

It was the big day—the day that the twins came home from the hospital. I wish I could say I was thrilled beyond belief, but at the very crux of my being, I was fucking terrified. In the hospital, we had a team of nurses and doctors at our disposal in case anything went wrong. At home, we were all on our own to somehow raise these two little lives. Of course, Abby was completely fearless when it came to the twins. She mastered breastfeeding the two of them at the same time, did great changing their diapers and giving them baths.

But me?

I was afraid that when I picked them up, I'd forget to support their head, causing them serious trauma. Or when I had to dress them or change their diaper, I feared pulling too hard on their arms or legs and having them fall off.

Oh yeah, I was a fucking basket case.

After what seemed like a small eternity, I got both Jax and Jules's car seats strapped in our new family-friendly SUV. Thankfully, they snoozed the entire time I cussed and worked up a sweat at getting them in right. They'd conked out shortly after Abby filled them up at feeding time just before we came downstairs.

After they were born, both of them faced a gamut of issues that prevented us from going home immediately. First, Jax turned jaundice. Then Jules had sucking reflex issues, so she started losing weight. This took a while to resolve. I had to give major props to Abby. She handled it all like a trooper as she tried getting Jules back on the breastfeeding train. Me, I would have just said screw it and given Jules a bottle. But Abby was determined to have the same bonding experience with Jules as she did with Jax. Like always, my Angel was amazing. Finally, Jules had hit the regulation five pounds to go home last night. We hadn't wanted to leave with Jax and not Jules.

I eyed the sleeping little angels, as Abby would call them, warily before I shut the door. I hoped they would continue sleeping this peacefully on the ride home. I didn't even want to begin to imagine what driving down the interstate with one screaming baby, least of all two, would be like. A thousand horrifying scenarios ran through my mind of me losing my shit in the car with the noise.

While there were all these maternal instincts that had kicked in for Abby the moment the twins were born, I hadn't experienced any paternal ones. Sure, I worried about them constantly when they were in the NICU, and all I wanted was them to be healthy and happy. But I still had yet to experience some overwhelming protective vibe, and that concerned me. Basically, I was totally fucking clueless when it came to the two little lives I'd helped create.

"Ready?" Abby asked, when I slid into the driver seat.

My hand hovered over the ignition before I glanced over at her. "Um, I don't think I'll ever be ready to take those two home with us."

She grinned. "It's going to be fine, Jake. *We're* going to be fine, and the *twins* are going to be fine."

"Deep down I know you're right. But I can't help feeling panicky whenever I think about the two of them and how we're completely responsible for them." I shook my head. "I can perform in front of fifty thousand people, and it doesn't scare me at all. But them," I jerked my thumb to the backseat, "they scare the hell out of me."

She rubbed my arm. "But we won't be all alone at first, babe. My mom and dad will be down at the barn if we need them. I mean, that's the plan of where they're staying, but if I know them, they'll be crashing on the couches to be closer to us and the twins."

"You won't hear me complaining."

It took us a little longer to get home considering I refused to go over the speed limit. Abby had fallen asleep when we got out of the city. I didn't bother waking her because I knew she needed her rest. When I finally turned the SUV into the driveway, I saw several cars lining the driveway. I pulled up to the front of the house and turned the car off. I leaned over to kiss Abby's cheek. "Wake up, Angel. We're home."

Her eyelids fluttered before she opened them. "Oh no, did I fall asleep?"

"It's okay. I didn't mind."

She smiled and brought her mouth to mine. "Thank you," she murmured against my lips.

"For what?"

"For making today possible. I've dreamed about it for so long. Do you know what an amazing feeling it is to be bringing our son and daughter home?"

I grinned. "Pretty damn amazing." I motioned to the door. "Let me get that for you."

"What a gentleman," she mused.

With a laugh, I hopped out of the door and came around the side for her. I opened the door and held out my hand to help her. "Jake, I'm not that fragile."

"Just humor me," I replied.

She put her hand in mine, and I helped her from the car. "Hi honey!" Laura called from the front porch.

"Hi Mom. Where's dad?"

"Oh he's taking Angel for a walk." Laura hurried down the stairs. "Need some help?"

"No, we're—" Abby began before I interrupted her.

"Can you get Jules's carrier?"

"Sure," Laura replied.

"I could have gotten her, Jake," Abby protested.

"I don't think so. Now go on and get in the house. You need to be off of your feet."

Abby rolled her eyes. "I thought once I had the twins you would stop being so overprotective."

I smiled and kissed her cheek. "Once you've recovered from the C-Section, you're all on your own."

She laughed. "I hope so."

As she started up the stairs, I opened the back seat. The twins stirred, but thankfully, they didn't start screaming. I passed Jules's carrier over to Laura before I went around to get Jax out. As I worked to release him, he peered up at me. "Hey buddy, you have a nice nap?"

His response was to flail his hands and poke out his tongue. As I stared into his face, I couldn't help seeing some of Abby in him. Sure, he had my dark hair, but the shape of his eyes, his nose, the dimple in his cheek—those were definitely her. Seeing a little mini-Abby made me smile.

I picked up the carrier and then started for the stairs. Rhys was standing at the bottom, grinning at me. "I didn't expect to see you here," I exclaimed, giving him a hug.

"Yeah, the guys and Mia and Lily wanted to surprise you. They're all inside. Brayden's helping Lily make lunch for you guys."

"That's awesome. Thanks."

"You need any help?"

"Uh, yeah, actually I do. Can you grab the diaper bag out of the back seat?"

His brows furrowed as he crossed his arms over his chest. "You want me to carry some purse thing?"

I laughed. "No one will revoke your man card, I promise. It's black, so it can be unisex for the twins."

"Fine," he grumbled, as he made his way over to the SUV. Once he had the diaper bag, he rejoined me, and we started up the stairs.

"So where are you headed on your break?" I asked.

"As much as I'd rather be shot, I'm heading down to Savannah to see the folks."

I grimaced as I thought of the two snobbish assholes who were Rhys's parents. A thought popped into my mind. "Hey man, while you're down there, can you check in on Allison?"

"Sure. But why?"

With a sigh, I thought of how my baby sister had broken down on me when she'd come up to see the twins. She was twenty now, and she was going to school in Savannah. "Her douchebag boyfriend broke up with her, and she's kinda down."

Rhys held open the door for me. "Heartbroken and away from home, huh?"

I nodded. "She needs to see a familiar face."

"Yeah, I'll call her up while I'm down there."

"Thanks, man, I appreciate it."

When we got inside, Andrew was in the living room with Angel on a leash. At the sight of us, she strained, wanting to get free.

I set Jax's carrier down on the floor next to Jules. "Wanna meet the babies, Angel?" Abby asked.

"I don't know if that is a good idea," Andrew said, holding firm to Angel's leash.

Abby's blonde brows furrowed. "And why not? She's a part of our lives and now the twins will be a part of hers."

Laura's forehead crinkled with worry. "I just think it would be best not to have a dog around the babies until they're a little older. Angel can just stay down at the barn with us."

"But I worked hard before the twins were born to get her used to the idea of a baby in the house, and she's the sweetest dog ever, so I know she wouldn't do anything to hurt them," Abby protested.

Andrew glanced over to me as if expecting me to put my foot down. He should have known that there was no way in hell, when Abby was less than two weeks off birthing two kids, that I was going to tell her no on anything, even if I thought it was the best not to have an eighty-pound dog slobbering over our newborns. When I just shook my head at him, he sighed. "Fine then." He unhooked the leash off of Angel's collar.

She made a beeline for the twins. My breath hitched when she stuck her nose into Jax's face. But she didn't try to bite his head off or anything crazy like that. She gave him a small lick on his hand before moving on to Jules. After she did the same thing to her, Angel hustled over to Abby. "Did you miss me?" Abby cooed.

Angel's tail went into a frenzy at the attention, and Laura and Andrew exhaled the breath they had been holding. With the worry of Angel out of the way, Andrew bent over Jax's carrier. "Mind if I hold my grandson?"

"Go right ahead," I said.

Andrew smiled as he unhooked Jax and then picked him up. As he gazed down at Jax, he smiled. "I think he looks a little bit like his mom."

"He does."

Laura grinned as she peeked at Jules. "But this one is going to be the spitting image of her daddy, I think."

My brows rose in surprise. "Really?"

Laura nodded. Abby abandoned Angel to come to my side. She snuggled against my chest and then jerked away. "Oh babe, you stink."

I laughed at her honesty. "Yeah, Jax puked on me this morning as I was getting him in the carrier."

"Why don't you go grab a shower?" When I opened my mouth to question her, she shook her head. "I think between the three of us, we have the twins covered."

"I want you lying down. Now," I commanded.

"Fine, fine," she muttered, before waltzing over to the couch. She made a big production of putting her feet up.

"Good. I won't be long."

Andrew patted Jax's back. "Take your time. We'll be fine."

I had just stepped out of a long, luxurious shower when Jules's piercing wail stopped me cold. I grabbed a towel and slung it around my waist before hauling it out of the bathroom. When I got into the bedroom, my gaze spun around the room before honing in on Laura who hovered over Jules on the bed.

"What are you doing to her?" I demanded over Jules's cries.

Laura jumped at my voice. With one hand still on Jules, she turned her head to look at me. "I'm only changing her diaper. Abby's feeding Jax."

"Then why is she crying like that?"

"I don't know." She gave me a knowing look. "Babies sometimes cry for no reason."

Even though I was still wet, I marched over to the bed. "Hey little girl, what's wrong?" As Jules kept crying, pain radiated through my chest. As soon as Laura taped up her diaper, I reached over to take Jules in my arms. She was so tiny that her butt fit into the palm of my hand as I cradled her against my damp chest. "Shh, it's okay, sweetheart. Daddy's here," I murmured into her ear.

Her cries began to quiet as I patted her back. As I rocked back and forth on my feet, Jules gave a contented little sigh. When I pulled my head back to eye her on my shoulder, I saw she was fast asleep.

"Guess she just wanted her daddy, huh?" Laura asked with a smile.

"That was…intense."

"Jake, you have to get used to their crying. They might keep you up all night with tummy troubles or teething."

"I know. It's just…" I was kinda afraid to tell Laura about how detached I had been feeling from the twins.

"It's what?" she pressed, crossing her arms over her chest.

"I think my paternal instincts finally kicked in."

"What do you mean?"

"Since the twins were born, I haven't felt as connected to them as Abby has. I've heard Brayden and AJ talk about that fierce, protective love they felt for their children, and I didn't exactly have that."

"Maybe you just had a delay."

My brows rose. "You think?"

She nodded. "With the twins in the NICU, you haven't had a chance to be around them like normal babies. After what happened with Jules in the delivery room, it's only natural that you've had your guard up worrying about them. That worry also erected somewhat of a wall to where you couldn't allow yourself to feel as much for them as you would like."

"It was Abby, too," I murmured.

Laura's forehead crinkled. "You were worried about something happening to her?"

"I was worried that if something happened to one or both of the twins, she wouldn't be able to handle it. I guess at first, I wanted them to live for her, not necessarily for me. Now that's changed." I gazed down at Jules and felt like my chest would explode from the overwhelming emotions coursing through me. "Everything's changed."

The old me would have been freaked out by that thought, but the new me—the one who was now a father—was pretty damn content. I didn't know how it would all work out, but deep down, I knew we would be fine. We'd be perfect.

Instead of my usual morning wake-up call of one or both of my babies crying, Jake's warm, moist lips kissed a trail up my neck and then over my chin. At the same time, his hand snaked over my hip to dip between my legs. Working me over my thin panties, I moaned and pressed myself back against him, feeling his heated desire burning against my leg.

Flicking my gaze to the antique clock on the nightstand, I knew we had about a ten minute window before the twins were awake and needing me. Turning over, I met Jake's frenzied kiss, his tongue darting eagerly into my mouth. When he pulled away to give me a wicked grin, my heartbeat accelerated in my chest. "Will you be okay with a quickie?" I murmured against Jake's lips.

"I'll take whatever you can give me, Angel."

"Hmm, then give me all you got."

So we wouldn't waste any time, Jake didn't even bother removing my pajama top. Instead, he did a one handed removal of my panties and tossed them over the side of the bed. He was out of his boxers in a flash. Since his hand had done a pretty good job getting me ready for him, he spread my thighs and nudged his erection at my center.

"Oh Angel, I love when you're so wet for me," he murmured, as he nuzzled his face into my neck.

I widened my legs and brought my hand between us to ease him home. When he was buried deep inside me, we both groaned with pleasure. While the twins continued sleeping soundly in the crib across from our bed, Jake pumped hard and furiously in and out of my body. Our roles of husband and wife were momentarily taking precedence over those of mommy and daddy. As I ran my hands over Jake's bare shoulders and back, our eyes remained locked on each other. The frequency of sex had certainly changed with the arrival of the twins, but when we were together, our connection was still as strong. It was something I knew I wanted to work on—I was a mother, but I was still Jake's wife. Since we had always had such a deep, physical connection, I wanted to continue making love to him as much as possible.

Although I knew Jake was close, my mind kept overriding my pleasure whenever I would feel the tingles begin. Sensing my need, Jake's hand reached between us, and his deft fingers sought out my swollen clit. He rubbed and tweaked it until I no longer trapped by my mind—I was completely surrounded by pleasure. "Jake!" I cried, as I tensed and came. He followed shortly with me.

After he was finished, we lay entangled in each other's arms. I drew lazy circles with my fingers over his taut back muscles. "Pretty good way to start a morning, huh?" he asked, breaking the silence.

I giggled. "I'd say so." Grasping at the strands of his hair, I tugged, pulling his face up to look at mine. "I love you, Jake."

"Mmm, I love you, too, Angel." He brought his lips to mine. Just as we were getting carried away again, Jax's agitated grunt came from the crib. It was shortly followed by a wail, and then Jules started in with him.

"Guess that's our cue," I said, after I broke off the kiss.

"You go get cleaned up from our morning exertions, and I'll get the hellions changed," Jake said.

I laughed. "Okay." As he rolled out of bed, I took in an appreciate eyeful of his delicious ass as he slid on his boxers. I then got up and padded over to the bathroom as Jake headed to the crib. For the moment, our bedroom was doubling as a second nursery. It just made more sense to have the twins close to us, rather than upstairs.

After I finished my morning business and cleaned up, I went back into the bedroom. My heart warmed at the sight of Jake standing over the crib, singing to the twins as he changed diapers. He was truly a sight to behold with all his muscles and tattoos. Of course, the twins were not appreciating his performance. Instead, they were wailing so loud that Angel began to howl along with them.

"Don't encourage them," I said to Angel, patting her on the head.

Once I was back in bed, I started unbuttoning my pajama top. Jake's singing ceased as he leaned over the crib's edge. "Shh, it's okay. Daddy's here, and he loves you," Jake murmured. No matter who was closest to the edge, he always picked Jules up first. I don't know if it was because she was tinier, the youngest, or he felt that protective Daddy vibe because she was his baby girl.

"That's my pretty little angel," he said. He tenderly kissed the top of her head before passing her over to me. We had two weeks to go before we were back on the road, and I had no idea how I would be able to keep breastfeeding like this. At almost four months, I felt they were more than ready to be weaned, but Jake was pretty insistent that at least Jules keep on as long as I could.

Once Jules latched on and nursed heartily, Jake picked up Jax. "Okay, chunky monkey," he said, with a grin to Jax's scrunched red face.

"Hey now, don't be giving him a weight complex," I chided.

"Ah, he's pure muscle, right Jaxy?" Jake asked, kissing our son's chubby cheek.

Since Jake had nothing to do with his feeding, Jax continued wailing as he strained for me. He outweighed Jules by a good five pounds. Whatever he'd had on her in the womb, he had maximized it now that he was out. Usually, we had to give him some formula after a feeding because he just never seemed to get enough. He was going to be built just like his dad when he grew up. But regardless of his size, he was terribly protective of Jules. Whenever they slept, he always laid as close as he could to her, and he wasn't satisfied unless he could touch her with his fist or feet.

Once Jax was in my arms, his cries quieted, and he snuggled in beside Jules to start feeding. Jake eased back into the bed. Lying on his stomach, he propped his head on his elbow and stared up at me. "You sure about going out on the road?"

I smiled. "Never more certain about anything. I can't wait to prove that I really am Wonder Woman, and I can be a Grammy-award-winning songwriter and performer, as well as a mother."

"Can I get you to wear a sexy Wonder Woman costume?" Jake teasingly asked.

"Maybe. If you play your cards just right," I replied, with a wink.

"I'll try my best."

"Keep doing what you're doing when it comes to helping me with the twins, and you'll get lots of nice rewards."

His brows then furrowed. "Do you really think Allison is going to be able to handle Jax and Jules?"

I laughed. "I think she's going to do the best she can. I mean, sometimes we have a difficult time handling them."

Jake's expression lightened. "That's true."

It had been hard deciding on a nanny or a babysitter for the twins. Jake and I both had been raised by very hands-on mothers, and I planned to be the same way, even when on tour. Having Allison along with us for the summer tour happened almost too divinely to believe. Since she was about to finish up her last semester at SCAD, or the Savannah School of Art and Design, she needed some internship and field experience in her major—fashion design. What better way to have her kill two birds with one stone than to have her work on costumes for Jacob's Ladder and Runaway Train while watching the twins during rehearsals and shows.

"I just hope your brothers don't get any ideas about her," Jake said, his fingers rubbing over one of Jax's crocheted booties that Mia had made him.

"I think they value their manhood too much to mess around with your baby sister," I replied, with a smile.

"They sure as hell better."

As I shifted Jax onto my shoulder to burp him, I resisted the urge to tell Jake that it wasn't my brothers and Allison he should be worried about. At the twins' christening, the unresolved sexual tension between Allison and Rhys was palpable. Something had definitely happened between them, but there was also a hell of a lot unsaid and unspoken going on. They worked their hardest to stay away from each other, but at the same time, they were constantly looking at each other. Since I wanted her along with us on the tour, I didn't dare pry. I knew the truth would come out when the time was right.

"What are you thinking about?" Jake asked.

"Nothing," I lied, diverting my gaze to Jules who had just finished eating.

"Oh, no, I saw that expression of yours—the one you get when the wheels in your head are turning."

"I'm just excited and nervous about the tour, that's all."

"We're going to be a full house on the bus with Allison and the twins."

"And Angel," I said. Hearing her name caused Angel to raise her head and wag her tail.

"You really think it's a good idea bringing her along?" Jake asked, as he took Jax from me, so I could burp Jules.

"I couldn't bear leaving her behind. Do you know what that would do to her if she saw us and the twins leaving her?"

Jake grimaced. He knew as well as I did that Angel was so attached to Jax and Jules. She slept at the foot of their crib every night. If we let one of them cry too long while trying to get their diaper changed or bottle ready, she started howling and barking. "Fine, fine, we'll bring Angel."

As Jules emitted a giant burp, I laughed. "Thank you, babe."

He shook his head. "I have no willpower when it comes to you."

"I know, and I love it," I teased.

Jake laughed. "Now that the little hellions—"

"Angels," I corrected.

"Fine. Now that the *angels* are fed, what's on tap for today?"

"Hmm, maybe baths for all of us, and then a nice, lazy movie day?"

"I like the sound of that. I bet I could get Papa to run down to Two Brothers for some BBQ for us."

My stomach growled appreciatively. "Yes, please."

Jake grinned. "Who would have ever thought my favorite things in the world would be lounging around in bed with my wife and kids?"

"You've come a long way since I first met you."

"And I have you to thank." He kissed Jax and then Jules. "And you two." Jax grinned while Jules seemed to reach out for Jake. As he took her into his arms, I couldn't help the happy tears that filled my eyes at the sight of Jake with his son and his daughter in his strong arms.

Jake sucked in a harsh breath. "What is it?" I asked.

He closed his eyes. "I'm getting another melody…oh yeah, definitely a new song."

"I'll get your guitar and notepad," I said.

This was our lives, after all. The music of our heart and soul.

The Pairing
Synopsis

After her former boyfriend left her pregnant and alone, Megan McKenzie swore off men. She spent the last eighteen months focused solely on her son, Mason, along with finishing nursing school at the top of her class. Although she's not ready to complicate her life with a long-term relationship, a nice no-strings attached hook-up is just what she needs. At her godson, Noah's, baptism, she finds the perfect candidate in the soft-spoken godfather, Pesh Nadeen. After all, the widower could use a good time too. But after drinking too much, the night doesn't end the way she thought it would. Forced to leave Pesh's house through a walk of shame, Megan hopes to never, ever see him again.

For Pesh Nadeen, the very sight of Megan sends him into an emotional tailspin. Since she reminds him too much of what he has lost, he wants to be out of her sight…at first. But the more he gets to know her, there's something about the diminutive blonde that causes his protective side to go into overdrive, and he finds himself wanting more. When Megan is assigned to him to complete her nursing clinicals, he sees it as fate, but she's having no part of it. She only wants a physical relationship while he wants far more.

What happens next is a sexy game of cat and mouse to see who will break first or if both of them will eventually get more than they ever bargained for.

Strings of the Heart
Synopsis

Twenty year old, Allison Slater has been in love with her brother's bandmate, Rhys McGowan, since she was fifteen years old. But to him, she'll always be Jake's little sister and off limits. Now a college sophomore and licking her wounds from a bad breakup, she sets her sights on making Rhys see her as someone he could date...maybe even love. Her opportunity comes when Rhys visits his parents in Savannah where she is attending college. But the night she's dreamed of turns to heart-break, and she realizes she'll never be the one for Rhys.

For Rhys McGowan, his nightmare began when he woke up, naked and hung-over, next to his bandmate's little sister. Unable to remember a thing from the previous night, he only makes matters worse by lying to Allison about not being interested in her. The truth is he's spent the last year to ignore his body's reaction whenever Allison is around. His resolve is tested when Allison comes on tour with Runaway Train, as both Jake and Abby's nanny and to fulfill her fashion design internship. The more time he spends with her in the close quarters of the bus, the harder it is for him to resist.

Will Rhys realize that having a relationship with Allison is worth fighting for even if it means that he has to fight his best friend for a chance?

About the Author

Katie Ashley is the New York Times, USA Today, and Amazon Best-Selling author of The Proposition. She lives outside of Atlanta, Georgia with her two very spoiled dogs and one outnumbered cat. She has a slight obsession with Pinterest, The Golden Girls, Harry

Potter, Shakespeare, Supernatural, Designing Women, and Scooby-Doo.

She spent 11 1/2 years educating the Youth of America aka teaching MS and HS English until she left to write full time in December 2012.

She also writes Young Adult fiction under the name Krista Ashe.

Follow Katie Ashley

Website

Facebook

Twitter

Goodreads

Amazon

Other Works of Katie Ashley

The Proposition | The Proposal | The Party

Music of the Heart | Beat of the Heart

Search Me | Don't Hate the Player...Hate the Game

Nets and Lies | Jules, the Bounty Hunter

The Guardians | Testament

CPSIA information can be obtained at www.ICGtesting.com
Printed in the USA
LVOW12s1917010514

384064LV00028B/877/P